THE GREAT INDIAN

MATRIMONIAL TAMASHA

notionpress.com

THE GREAT INDIAN MATRIMONIAL TAMASHA

HIMIKA GANGULY

notionpress.com

Notion Press

Old No. 38, New No. 6

McNichols Road, Chetpet

Chennai - 600 031

First Published by Notion Press 2016

ISBN 978-93-5206-725-1

To all who are a part of it, I understand your pain.

To all who are not a part of it, if your story was pleasurable enough, you would not be reading mine.

Contents

Chapter 1
The Woman's Man Challenge

So I see one of my last extra virgin, extra independent and no rules for life friend announce that she has finally found her—THE MAN. At the place where I am and I am sure many others just like me are immediately realize that this THE MAN is a million times more indispensable and harder to find than HE MAN.

HE MAN had the Power of the Universe. But THE MAN has the power to switch the pause button on the biological clock trauma taunts that most unmarried girls in the age bracket of 25–35 are made to hear, silence once and for all our father's aunt's uncle's neighbour's sister's cousin's great grandma whose last Deepawali wishes included sweet barfis, a sweeter phone call and the very sweet laced acid question—so did your daughter finally find the man of her dreams?

Who said we need paranormal activity to evoke nightmares. The question of the availability of the man of our dreams does it for our entire family. Amazing success rate. We are two weeks down.

Coming back to the most important part of this story. Me. Since any of you haven't seen me yet, except those amazing friends who have contributed to the noble cause of increasing my book's sales, trust me you secure a place in heaven for this one act; I am pretty. Not very pretty, but yes, the necessary pretty. I am an MBA in marketing and a post graduate diploma in advertising management and public relations from one of the finer colleges of this country. I am a hit in the social network circuit and an average in the party scene for which I hold my Bengali Bhaalo Mein (good girl) rule book solely responsible. Though I must mention here, some Bengalis which includes me to a very outsized extent are certainly a few of the nicest people in the world. I have a liberal father and an extremely caring mother who at this moment is wondering why her hair is rapidly greying and thyroid levels massively jumping. She calls it menopause. I think it is the bin bihaayi beti syndrome. That apart I work in an MNC and handle the brand. I also cook. Great friends, greater vacations, some money and such is life. A good life!

Now some of you reading this book must have accepted the fact that I am not at the top yet but certainly somewhere closer to the Everest of happiness. Many must be also deciding—okay loud single bitch…trying so hard to prove her point of perfection.

But there…those who matter. The last few rare pearls who must have got the point. She mentioned that she would speak about herself. But, so far, all the vocabulary was about work, education, her skill set and her parents; who are like any other parents.

Why not a word about her, the woman?

This is exactly the point where the tamasha begins. In matrimonial business, you don't matter. Or you do but that is so much later. What strikes you off or gives you a thumbs up are rather some very typical, important nevertheless but easily manipulative points. Here is an example.

A typical matrimony site will see a profile of the following nature.

Boy's photo (the ugly ones either don't put any pictures or put too many pictures with the darkest glares that hide their hideousness).

Profile created by (mother/father/brother/sister/sister-in-law/friend—often the decision making's maximum rights are allotted to this candidate)

Boy's height—Whatever it may be, in most cases, it happens to be below the stated statistics.

Boy's education—Often right. Some occasions exaggerated.

Boy's salary—Often the range is mentioned. Like 15–20 lakhs or 25–40 lakhs or 3–5 lakhs. Like a few lakhs don't matter really right! Ask me.

Boy's family—A tall verbose on greatness and legacy fitting for the king. Though some do sell modesty as well.

Boy's weight—This is such a dynamic parameter, but anyways.

Place of Birth—Matchmaking purpose

Time of Birth—Matchmaking purpose

Date of Birth—Matchmaking purpose

When my parents got married nobody really cared. They lived happily ever after without the horoscope matching business. But the India, we live in today, which by the way out of the many evils it allows to breed, continues to let another dark and monstrous practice survive and flourish. No no it is not astrology. Astrology still has some science to it.

It is the Ekta Kapoor serial business.

Her kundali matchmaking and lavish weddings and marriages not working unrealistic plots have aggravated the scene and have brought horoscopes back in fashion. I am sure if not the gods; then at least astrologers around the world must have blessed her for that.

Anyways along with these columns, there are questions like does the boy smoke or drink, which normally has either a 'big yes' or a 'big no' or most often an 'occasionally' to it. Again, a frivolous measure.

And finally, the matter of concern is- the expectations from the girl. I often read the following line. Should be career oriented and at the same time homely and respectable towards elders. I get the career and respect bit, but that point of homeliness is somewhere in grey.

Then the age of the girl and her qualifications are set which again don't look very serious.

So now you see, what I mean by talking about me. In a regular dot com website with marriage as the selling product, 'I' is never really about me. It is how strong is the bank balance, what I might look like and finally what I need you to be like vaguely.

It is an odd task and often some get lucky, whereas many don't. What does happen in the process is you meet so many different minds that there comes a point when you lose the little sanity left and start writing about the odd ones.

Yes, I have arrived at a point where I can be deemed a recluse.

I have lost interest in manhood at the moment.

My friends are asking me if I am turning homosexual.

My sincere reply—no, I am not homosexual or heterosexual. I am a no sexual at the moment.

From next page onwards, I will write the kahaanis of all those who are responsible for making the once full of life, giggles and passion personified Bengal ki Rani to a Pyaali of chai that's flavourless with too much paani.

Chapter 2

BMW Dreams of an Aeroplane Mistri

I prefer to go backwards and speak of a recent tragedy that is fresh in my mind. This is the latest piece I tested in one of the more thriving and crowded matrimonial malls of the current marketplace.

So Mr Aeroplane Mistri contacted us over a mail. And on the face of it, he seemed pretty acceptable and if I may say sober. Mom was particularly thrilled. With his white uniform and cap she imagined her daughter immediately as the dashing woman's darling pilot's wife which is not a bad thing. Then, of course, her hopes dampened a bit when she saw his profession column. Aircraft engineer. Okay you can have a piece of the cake if not entire.

Cockpit na sahi, plane ka paiyya hi sahi.

Pilot na sahi, uske uniform mein engineer hi sahi.

A house in one of the better suburbs of the city was one of the key USPs of this product. He looked a little short of hair, but who says bald men can't shine? And then you win some, you lose some.

By now I had figured out this trade well enough. The first phone conversation was enough to decode that this was not The Man. But we choose to try. And ignore. And try again.

So when Aeroplane Mistri called the first time, I knew that there was no light at the end of this tunnel. In fact, I did not want to enter this tunnel at all.

Bad English is such a turn off!

Aeroplane Mistri—So, how are you?

Bengal Rani (me)—I am good, you say.

Aeroplane Mistri—Nothing just going to the gym. I like gyming. I gym a lot. I am very high on weights. I drink protein shake every day. I love gyming. It is my life. You like gyming?

Bengal Rani (clearly wondering why the gym love confession was uttered anyways)—Okay, I prefer yoga.

Aeroplane Mistri—Ya yoga is not bad. But you should do weights. Weights are better. Come to my gym and I will teach you how to do weights.

Bengal Rani (uncomfortable with each passing microsecond)—Let's see. So, have you been staying in Mumbai for a long time?

Aeroplane Mistri—My father was IAS officer in Delhi. We shifted later. But what power we saw in Delhi. I used to go to Rashtrapati Bhavan with him and big politicians used to bow and do a Namaste to my father. My father is a family friend of big industrialists.

Bengal Rani (now beginning to realize that Delhi has a hand in this)—Oh nice to hear that. You must be very proud of your father!

Aeroplane Mistri—Of course, my father is a hero. So what about you? You have a tattoo?

Bengal Rani (not sure if she heard it right)—Excuse me?

Aeroplane Mistri—You have a tattoo? Tattoo I said? Where do you have the tattoo?

Bengal Rani (after hearing every word of the question and convincing herself that this too shall pass)—Sorry, I don't think I would like to answer that question.

Aeroplane Mistri (now quickly understanding that this was a wrong one)—Sure sure. You are the lady and you can decide to say or not to say. So tell me about work. What work you do? Bengal Rani (chanting Om Namah Shivay, dear lord save me in mind, body and soul)—I am into marketing communications. So branding, events, social media and public relations are part of my portfolio.

Aeroplane Mistri—Corporate. I have shift job. My life is very exciting.

Bengal Rani—Good. So is mine. Aeroplane Mistri—Very good dear.

Bengal Rani (quickly sensing the escape route)—Sure. Okay my boss is calling. I will speak to you later. Take care.

Aeroplane Mistri—Okay you call me when you are free again. We must keep talking.

Bengal Rani (trying hard to be polite)—Sure. Goodbye.

Aeroplane Mistri—Bye.

The phone goes off and at that moment I really begin to experience what Gandhiji explained years back—Silence is golden.

Thankfully, the first call was in between a workday with no immediate verdicts to give out to the family. However, later that would have to happen. But, for now, I could at least go back to life and forget this incident.

The day progressed in great shape and by evening I was happy that the Wednesday sudden dinner plan was on its way and in the next two hours.

The very air of Le Pain Quotidian was so inviting. Good French food has always lifted my moods and the day was more good than bad. And then friends were always the best things that happened to life. So while the chatter rang high, the wine went deep and the bruschetta along with stroganoff filled the belly and satiated the taste buds…the phone rang.

Aeroplane Mistri calling.

I am basically nice like most normal people. Hence, instead of disconnecting the call, I pick and tell the person on the other end that I am busy. You can follow this habit of mine. But, however, you must keep in mind what I learnt that day over the phone sitting in my favourite restaurant.

Bengal Rani (taking the call)—Hi. Aeroplane Mistri—So, how is it going?

Bengal Rani (keeping courtesy alive)—Very good. Hope you are good too.

Aeroplane Mistri—Oh I am fantastic.

Bengal Rani—Sure. Okay just wanted to tell you that I am out with friends over dinner at the moment. So can we speak later?

Aeroplane Mistri—So what? You can still talk to me. So what if they are around?

Bengal Rani (receiving her second shock of the day from the same source. The tattoo wound is still in memory)—No, not really. I need to give them time.

Aeroplane Mistri—But you need to give me time too.

Bengal Rani—We can speak later. I am with people and I feel uncomfortable talking in front of people please.

Aeroplane Mistri—Really? Is it that difficult for you? You can give it a try.

Bengal Rani (now out of patience and not courtesy abiding)—Sorry.

Aeroplane Mistri—Cool. So you call me when you are free okay.

Bengal Rani—Yes I will. Tomorrow afternoon. Aeroplane Mistri—I shall wait.

Bengal Rani—Thanks. Goodnight.

And finally back to the awesome friendly chatter that affirms that if silence is golden, gossip is platinum with diamond engravings.

Saloni asks me who was it and I shrug off my shoulders. She gets the message.

Saloni—You know it will not stop till we finally say yes.

Bengal Rani—You too?

Saloni—We both are nice looking twenty-nine-year-old unmarried women. Are you expecting it to be any different? But yes I have finally announced it at home.

Bengal Rani—What? I thought you didn't like the guy who has been asking you out.

Saloni (with that exasperated expression)—Which guy! Anyways, doesn't matter. I have announced. Get the guys. If I like, I will marry. If I don't, no questions. If I never like, I am happily single. Full stop.

Her braveries impress me though I could never still get myself to do this. Saloni and I connect really well, but yes we are different people.

Saloni—But yes, I spoke to a guy yesterday and rejected him over the phone call.

Bengal Rani—Why? Is he that bad?

Saloni—Weird. When we started talking for the first few minutes, roughly fifteen, he did a presentation on the benefits of Mumbai metro.

Bengal Rani—Did you reject him for that? Too much, don't you think?

Saloni—No. I am sane. I asked him a question. His answers were unlike any other man.

Bengal Rani (with a playful smirk)—He must be unique Saloni. Not a bad thing!

Saloni—I asked him what his favourite hobby is. He replied—I like decorating the house, shopping during sale season and talking to friends over the phone.

No further questions were asked. We ate our Apple Pie with the rest of the group of which two are dating, one is married and cursing his state of current affairs, the fourth actually happily married for a month now and the fifth who has a husband and a boyfriend.

Every morning, I hope that the question will not be asked. Every morning, my hopes are shattered.

Mom—You want oats?

Bengal Rani—Let me think.

Mom—Did he call?

Bengal Rani—Yes we spoke.

Mom—How is he?

Bengal Rani—Let's see.

Mom—You did not like him too much?

Bengal Rani—I am not saying that. He has a good job and a very powerful father I understand. Must be good.

Mom (the mood changes and with a big smile)—Should I make fried eggs for you? I know that you like them so much.

Bengal Rani—Actually, oats will do.

Mom—Are you sure?

Bengal Rani—Yes. And I have a meeting early today.

Mom—No problem. You will do well. By the way, when are you meeting him?

Bengal Rani—Let him decide. He will ask and then I shall tell you.

Mom—Alright…but try this weekend. Will be good. You also need to go out. Why should you sit at home?

Bengal Rani—My friends are going to Sula this weekend. Can I go there instead?

Mom—I will get your oats. Do what you want. It is your life.

For the rest of the world, this might be a very strange conversation. For every girl undergoing the matrimony saga, this is just another day. Just another mummy beti chit chat.

As I head out of home, I count the number of days till weekend. Of course, I will have to keep the promise of the call. And I hope, he also promises himself or any God he believes in to not say something that will put me off again.

The dreaded afternoon comes really quick. Technically 12 pm is afternoon and so is 4 pm. It is 4.30 pm. Can't avoid any longer.

Bengal Rani dialled Aeroplane Mistri. As expected, he picked the call within the first two rings.

Aeroplane Mistri—Yes madam…you finally got time to call.

Bengal Rani—Yes, I had a busy day.

Aeroplane Mistri—You should take an off and sit at home. You are a corporate slave.

Bengal Rani (this is the most hateful statement ever made to a woman who loves her work)—Excuse me, do you own your business?

Aeroplane Mistri—No, but I am a master of my work. I do as I wish.

Bengal Rani (now infuriated)—And I love my work. I get to meet the best in the industry and do some of the most interesting work. I meet the most influential people around and get to create a story for the brand that is phenomenal. And I have access to the cream of this country. Perks of a white collared job you see!

Aeroplane Mistri (hurt enough to finally utter the most stupid statement)—Good for you. So now, that you are dating an airlines person, you must know something about airlines.

Bengal Rani (unable to make sense of what was just communicated)—What? Dating?

Aeroplane Mistri—Yes.

Bengal Rani—We are not dating. We are talking matrimony. This is not dating.

Aeroplane Mistri—One and the same. Okay, let's meet this weekend.

Bengal Rani (cursing but now sure to finish this soon)—Sure. Sunday then, at the Aromas Coffee Shop in Santacruz.

Aeroplane Mistri—Alright. What time?

Bengal Rani—Six sharp. And I have relatives coming. So I won't have much time.

Aeroplane Mistri—One hour at least? You should at least give me that much time.

Bengal Rani (feeling helpless)—Okay. Bye now. Have work.

Aeroplane Mistri—Bye. I shall see you soon.

Two days later, D day arrives. Mom and dad look hopeful. That is not a nice thing.

Mom—You are not looking very fair today.

Bengal Rani—He is dark anyways. Doesn't matter.

Mom—Can you please see the good in him?

Bengal Rani—I am going to see the good and the bad. Do you mind?

Mom—Best of luck my child. I will pray for you.

Bengal Rani (leaving home rather tired)—I am going to meet a guy. Not on war. Bye!

Within minutes, Aeroplane Mistri's name flashes as incoming call on my phone. He has not been able to find Aromas Coffee shop. I don't bother to explain much but politely give directions as much as I can and when he still does not understand pat comes the common standard answer—use Google maps.

His first look isn't bad. He looks better than I expected. However, the conversation is so alarming that you will now finally know why he is not in my future must haves.

Aeroplane Mistri (settling down in the coffee shop on the chair, his well question one)—So how do you find me?

Bengal Rani—Ya okay fine.

Aeroplane Mistri—I look good. See I told you I work out.

Bengal Rani (looking at the watch)—I have ordered. Do you want me to order something for you?

Aeroplane Mistri—Yes Cappuccino (he pronounces it wrongly).

Bengal Rani—Did you have trouble in parking your car?

Aeroplane Mistri—Not much. I like driving. In the next two years, I will drive a better version of BMW. You see I earn two lakhs a month. That is good right!

Bengal Rani (sighing at another show off statement)—Sure. What about your house that is getting constructed?

Aeroplane Mistri—Two years possession. Some dispute with the builder. Do you like partying?

Bengal Rani (thanking her stars that the cappuccino and mojito have finally arrived)—Kind off. Why?

Aeroplane Mistri—I party all the time. Few days back I was at Olive, Lower Parel. Blew fifty thousand rupees there.

Bengal Rani (drinking her mojito fast)—Good for you. Do you have any aims in life?

Aeroplane Mistri—Life goes on. I am doing well. No regrets.

Bengal Rani (gulping the last sip of her drink)—I am a very independent person let me tell you. I love my work and I don't allow anyone to decide for me—clothes, etc. I wear my shorts and skirts.

Aeroplane Mistri—Even I wear shorts and skirts…oops I mean shorts.

Thankfully my phone rings.

Bengal Rani (to the caller who is her best friend)—Yes, I will be free in fifteen minutes. Yes let's meet.

Then looking at Aeroplane Mistri I explain, "My friend is flying to New York next week. I need to meet her."

Aeroplane Mistri—No problem. You are blushing. Just say you like me.

Bengal Rani (now amused so much that almost bursts out laughing)—Excuse me, you are thinking too fast and too much. I have no such things in my head. I will let you know. My friend will arrive. May I leave?

Aeroplane Mistri (now pushing too hard and noticing that I don't look interested)—She hasn't come yet. So let's go and chat inside my car.

Bengal Rani (getting up)—Not really. Some other time maybe. Not today.

Aeroplane Mistri (feeling hopeful again that all is not lost yet)—Okay as you wish. Will you call me?

Bengal Rani—When I am free I will. Thanks and have a great evening.

Saying this much I bid farewell to the over enthusiastic, apparently twenty-five lakhs a year earning, thirty-one-year-old prospect who worked in the airlines industry, knew nothing about Google maps, considered speaking equivalent to dating, asked absurd questions, spoke broken English, never read Economic Times, had no interests in anything that comes close to the term called knowledge and understood only one aspect of life—gyming.

Needless to say, Aeroplane Mistri called again and again and again. But his calls were either answered too coldly or not replied to at all.

What was wrong with him?

Do I really need to answer that question!

If you haven't got it yet, then either you are too innocent an angel.

Or too dumb a donkey.

Chapter 3
I Like Small, You too Must

The beginning like all other beginnings was good. It is the story ahead that changes the end anyways. Always.

I was so impressed with my dear mother. She was on the lookout forever and no promising profile could escape her ever attentive eagle eyes. Through this entire search, I have learnt one very important lesson of life. The world may give up on you but not your parents. They will try to get you the best. Often, they feel very defeated that their judgment of best was not particularly right. However, they don't give up. And if for nothing else, we better be thankful for the final force behind this entire struggle. Pure love which is.

When mom showed the profile to me, I was happy. Degrees from the international top notch universities, and a job in one of the best organizations in the world. This looked like the man of my dreams. At least on paper.

He did not look bad either. And had done a fair bit of travelling which is in my line of interest too. The only hitch was that he stayed in another city, which is not very far from mine. So we discussed and mom said that possibly I could go to and fro and do some weekend visiting and three years or so later a better plan could be chalked out. She understood my will to work and appreciated it more than I realized.

So IT Saab's parents were visiting Mumbai soon to get an ailment treated that his father was suffering from for a very long time. They called and invited us to visit them at well…the hospital. First setback was this.

However, we complied. Maybe his father was in a seriously bad state, and it would be only very kind of us to go and see them.

That evening, we left home to meet a matrimonial proposal at the pre decided location called- Ranavati hospital. The sound of it was bizarre though.

IT Saab greeted us, as we entered the room where his father was resting. I liked him the first time. He looked decent. Not great but the necessary decent. Moreover, he had a sober appearance.

IT Saab—So sorry, you had to come here. Father is unwell. Spinal cord problem.

Dad—It's absolutely alright. We understand. (then looking at IT Saab's father) How is your health sir?

IT Saab's father (in a very feeble voice)—Health is something that God decides on. We are mere humans after all. As long as he lets us live, we will live. Then I hope heaven has a place for me.

IT Saab's mother (quickly interrupting)—Don't say that. You will live many more years hale and hearty. (then looking at my mom)—He used to be fit. One day, he was playing cricket and running between the wickets. The ball hit the stumps much before he could get himself ahead of the line. He did not accept and refused to budge from the field. My brother let him have his way and then in the very next ball while running between the wickets, he had a very bad fall backwards. Since then he has been like this. Karma I tell you. He should have accepted his defeat.

IT Saab's father—I was not out. And it was my land on which the match was being played upon. You have more to say?

Dad (trying to lighten the mood decided to strike a conversation with IT Saab)—So son, what have you been up to?

IT Saab—Uncle I studied in London for years and now of course work is taking a good amount of time. There is a lot of work.

IT Saab's mother (now beginning her set of questions)—So can you sing?

Bengal Rani (immediately remembering that the parents actually belong to Bhubaneswar)—No sorry. I sing only film songs and English sometimes.

IT Saab's mother (not impressed and moving to question two)—Can you dance?

Bengal Rani (wondering if they will ask for a demo now)—Yes I can do belly dancing and zumba. IT Saab's mother (looking crestfallen and moving to question three immediately)—Can you cook?

Bengal Rani (thankfully a question that is in affirmative territory)—Yes I can. In fact I do.

IT Saab's mother looks happy for now and asks IT Saab to order tea. I think that evening my culinary skills degree won us our cups of tea.

Tea was rather quiet and I noticed IT Saab's phone and mannerisms. His father continued his heroic legends of how he moved an ancestral sofa that was equivalent to mountains, rivers and worlds alone with his bare hands when the back was better. We like courteous guests listened solely because the product looked promising and the spineless father and the henna hair laden mother were not a part of this package deal. He stayed away from them.

Anyways, the meeting ended on a not so bad note. And we exchanged numbers.

Now here is where the tamasha starts.

A day later I called IT Saab. I am positive this time. From what things looked like last time, this product looks promising.

IT Saab finally picks the call after five rings.

IT Saab—Hellooo (no matter what, accent is one thing a lot of men don't get right)

Bengal Rani (optimistic that there will be other things that will be nice and to smile about at the end of the call)—Hi. How are you? Is it a good time to speak?

IT Saab—Actually I am taking my mother around to show her the city.

Bengal Rani—Oh I am so sorry. No problem, we may speak some other time.

IT Saab—Wait, what I can do is that when the bus stops I will call you. Bengal Rani—Bus?

IT Saab—Yes, Mumbai Darshan bus.

Bengal Rani (a bit jolted)—Okay, you could have booked a car or rental taxi for a day. It would have been much more convenient, don't you think? Moreover, from what dad said, you have lived in this city for a long time.

IT Saab—Yes, I have. But why spend unnecessarily. Everything is anyways publicly available and whatever is free should by all means be considered. Small and low cost living is crucial to live a happy, uncomplicated life. You too must remember this since we are talking about life together. Bengal Rani (picking the hints and doing a character sketch mentally)—Sure. Hope your father is better now.

IT Saab—Very good news there. One his health is improving and two we could shift him from double sharing to triple sharing. Isn't that wonderful!

Bengal Rani (totally sure about why he is so ecstatic about the shift)—Yes of course. So you continue. We can speak later.

IT Saab—Okay. Take care.

Bengal Rani—Bye.

The goodness of golden silence. Thought reaffirmed. Thank you, Gandhiji. First for this, and then for freedom.

So the hope balloon has suddenly begun to lose air. Though it is full to quite an extent, but a chubby full blown balloon to a limp one, you know the difference.

Just when I am pondering and trying to see some good in what I heard, Alisha my junior settles into a vacant seat right next to me and gives me a soft pat to break my thoughts.

Alisha—You think a lot you know.

Bengal Rani—No baby, I am just relaxing.

Alisha—How bad is he?

I smile and pity the moment. Maybe I am too expressive off late. Maybe it is not a very good thing. However, Alisha who is a year younger has her story to tell and this time she too is hoping to find a listening ear. You know there are some who strongly believe in talking, letting it out and off with it. It is a great formula and I am experimenting with it lately. If nothing else, it is hormone balancing surely. My skin feels even unlike the last few months for a proof.

Alisha—I have to tell you about this guy I spoke to last few days.

Bengal Rani—Tell me. I sincerely hope your story is better than mine.

Alisha—No way. What do you do with a man obsessed with himself?

Bengal Rani—What do you do with a man obsessed with saving?

Alisha—Ask him to save himself for something more substandard.

I laugh. This bit of satire is exactly what I needed and I know Alisha well enough to be capable of that kind of sudden sunshine.

Alisha—So here is Mr Awesome. Studying in one of the top MBA colleges of the world and in love with himself.

Bengal Rani—Isn't that good in a way? To be happy and satisfied with yourself?

Alisha—Limits are necessary. I will tell you how he speaks.

"Hey, you know I am doing this fantastic study on human buying behaviour and I know my professor is so going to love it. You know I am awesome."

"So we are planning camping in the woods tonight. And we shall walk it up from university to deep inside the woods and I shall be leading things. You see, you know I am awesome."

"So it rained yesterday here. And I just felt like doing something different. So I went up and cooked something like dal. Wow, you know I am awesome."

"Yes, I did have a girlfriend for two weeks or so I think. But it did not quite last. Can't call her a girlfriend really. You know. I am awesome."

Alisha—So you see, he was so awesome and I did give him chances all through the week, then I finally said that hey dude, you are not really awesome enough for me. Bye.

Bengal Rani (with her eyes wide open)—Such men actually exist? Really, I am losing faith in humanity.

Alisha—Unfortunately, they do. And in the matrimonial world they blossom their worst best. Anyways I have decided.

Bengal Rani—What? To say no to boys?

Alisha—That will not help. Moreover I do not have a problem with boys. I like boys. They are a necessity you know. (she grins to that devilishly)

Alisha—I have a plan to get my scholarship in place for my study and PhD somewhere in the Nordic region. That way, I will not face this nuisance, stay away and finally get the firang I have always had my eyes on.

Bengal Rani—That is a plan. Are you prepared?

Alisha—More than ever. This is my only chance.

Bengal Rani—All the best. Hope you flee soon.Alisha (getting up and winking)—If I can I will pass on the details to you. Who knows, we both may find our respective firangs together.

The hope and will of the woman today. Alisha is one small example of the changing scenario of the fairer sex and its perceptions in a fast changing world. There was a time when it was first husband only. Then it changed to first husband and then PhD if workable along with it. And today there is a third transference of definitely PhD and boyfriend/husband/fling, etc. if workable along with it. The right and wrong of it can be debatable. But the denial of it happening is preferable blindness.

By evening I am set to go for my meditation classes. Yoga and meditation classes actually, but today is a day just right for meditation. A cup of green tea, some twenty minutes before meditation, is a bliss moment. As I am nibbling my bliss situation piece by piece, the phone rings.

IT Saab calling. Suddenly my elevated moods felt on an uneven plane. I am not feeling prepared for this call. But I have to take it I think.

Bengal Rani—Hello

IT Saab—Hellooo. How are you?

Bengal Rani (realizing that the tone reminds of great grandma)—I am good. How are you? And how was your Mumbai sightseeing?

IT Saab—What sightseeing? Mumbai has only sea, sea and sea to see.

Bengal Rani (did not like those words against her favourite city)—Yes, but still Mumbai is a beautiful place.

IT Saab—I don't agree. It is only for banking and finance people.

Bengal Rani—No not just that. It is also the hub of advertising.

IT Saab—Are you trying to say that advertising happens only in Mumbai?

Bengal Rani—There can be sub-agencies and agencies in other cities. I am not denying that. All I am saying is that Mumbai is the hub of the advertising and media world.

IT Saab—I don't agree with you.

Bengal Rani—I think I can say this much as it is my field.

IT Saab—You think I don't know anything about advertising? (he is getting rude)

Bengal Rani—I did not say so. I just said that I will know about my area of work.

IT Saab—I have friends who work in agencies in other cities. One of my friends owns an advertising agency in a small city. Big IT companies come to him for work.

Bengal Rani (clearly, trying hard to not raise her volume and temper)—I said there are agencies in other cities. My point is of majority.

IT Saab—You do not know your field properly then.

Bengal Rani—What?

IT Saab—I will mail you my email ID. Find reports and prove me what you said.

Bengal Rani (now feeling extremely beaten, hopeless and desperate to bang his head into the laptop)—I don't think I want to do that. Anyways, this topic is not taking us anywhere. Let's change it.

IT Saab—Okay. As you wish. But first tell me. How important do you attribute values to this media business of yours?

Bengal Rani (this media business of yours! Death of respect)—It is a very important part of our business. Why do you ask that?

IT Saab—The news channels you work with are so unethical. I feel your people have no value system.

Bengal Rani—News channels are also a reason why you get to know what happens in this country at such a short span of time. I think it is best to focus on the brighter aspects of things. If we really debunk every sector, then frankly wherever there will be business, there will be a question on values and ethics.

IT Saab—So you are saying sensationalizing is ethical?

Bengal Rani—No it might not be. But every story is not sensationalized and majority of the news is serious in nature.

IT Saab—Okay, in that case let's talk about you. Will you accept the job of a brand manager for an alcohol brand?

Bengal Rani—If the money is good, then why not. It is a high investment industry where marketing spends have been flamboyant.

IT Saab—And if you were to become brand manager for a cigarette brand then?

Bengal Rani—I doubt I would. I am personally not fond of smoking as a practice and moreover what if the product falls under the ban curse? Hence, I might not take it up. But I cannot be sure. Will decide when I have to. If I have to.

IT Saab—See you are such a confused person with no sense of direction.

Bengal Rani (cursing him in mute mode nonstop)—I think I have answered your question. And anyways why are you taking my interview?

IT Saab—No I am not. See I am an MBA from a very good college and I believe group discussions are the best way to decode a person.

Bengal Rani—Okay I have a meeting. We shall speak some other time.

IT Saab—Okay. Have a great evening. Bye.

I disconnected the call. Whatever was great about the evening has definitely fizzled out for now.

I call up my Art of Living teacher and he laughed it off like every time. "Just be and flow" is his universal mantra for everything. According to him, I am trying too hard and pushing myself too much. He asks me to enjoy idiots, meet them, make them pay my food bills and then do as I wish. I find his advice amusing and I am doing it for now. It is like a revenge for the grief they bring. Sweet revenge. Though Karma has been watching and like the third law of motion the reaction is very visible on the weighing scale.

For the next two days, I am out for an offsite. The best thing about offsites is that it gives you a chance to disconnect. So I have blocked IT Saab's number for two whole days. I can always go back and say bad network.

We are a team of thirty-five people in this offsite, and we are here for an experiential training. I land up meeting an absolutely amazing single mother who is one of the prime trainers there. Sara is a forty-year-old talented woman who is busy in making good money and raising her ten-year-old son Lakshya. I often get chances to speak to her in between and after the training and find her words very encouraging.

Sara has experienced her personal hell of sorts. But she is not a product of self-pity. In fact her favourite line that I gathered in the last two days is—we all have our personalized and tailor-made heavens and hells.

On day three when we are leaving, Sara bids me farewell, we promise to trouble each other over WhatsApp each day and then she kisses my cheek and says something I will never forget—There is wisdom in your speech. Don't let it die.

I don't see a challenge with that. But I see a challenge now. We are back to reality and there is IT Saab's number to unblock. As I do so, I reassure myself, this too shall pass.

Tonight my parents are just too happy to have me back and my mother is excited as two more promising proposals have arrived. So no questions were asked. Dad tried to know if IT Saab and I have been talking, and I said a half-hearted yes. They are in peace with that for now.

Next morning.

I am so looking forward to the morning today. The training has helped me recognize my strengths. I am aware of my weaknesses but needed a closer introduction with some of my strengths which I did not realize were a part of me all this time.

Suddenly my mom comes storming inside my room with a small rosary of tiny beads in her hands and puts it around my neck.

Mom—There...see the design is perfect. Less is more you keep saying. See just like the clothes you wear, this too is small and tiny.

Bengal Rani—I do not approve of this.

Mom—I do not approve of those clothes you wear either.

Bengal Rani—My body, my clothes, my choice.

Mom—My daughter, my responsibility, my choice.

Bengal Rani—That was a very forced choice of words.

Mom—Listen girl, I am being patient enough. While you eat to glory, I stay hungry for you. While you rap to the tunes of that funny jumping bald man (she's talking about Pitbull), I chant Om Namah Shivay and Hare Rama Hare Krishna. While you throw money on expensive makeup, I save money and give it to astrologers to make up your destiny with the right poojas. Now, will you wear this? I need to call the Panditji, the senior Panditji suggested.

Reluctantly I put it on. Sometimes choice doesn't exist. Moreover it cost her two thousand rupees she informs. It will apparently ward off evil. Wasn't pepper spray supposed to do that until last week?

Apart from the morning drama which is a regular phenomenon, the day passes smoothly and the call doesn't come. In fact, I met a very good friend for lunch who tries hard to explain the necessity of a diet chart while we tear down and gobble burgers loaded with cheese, mayo and huge chunks of chicken together.

They say that calamity strikes unexpected. And the rule is very apt. So my phone rings and there I see. IT Saab is calling. My friend, whom I have enlightened about this particular incident, nudges me to put the phone on speaker. For second advice sake, I accepted the idea.

IT Saab—How are you? Where were you the last two days? I had called.

Bengal Rani—Hi, I was on an offsite. I think my phone was unreachable.

IT Saab—So don't you think it is your responsibility to inform me before you leave as I might try calling?

Bengal Rani—Did you try?

IT Saab—That is irrelevant. You should have informed. Anyways, I need to talk to you.

Bengal Rani—Sure. Go on.

IT Saab—What do you think of Bombay?

Bengal Rani—I think it is Mumbai.

IT Saab—My question is about what do you think of the city you live in?

Bengal Rani—I think it is the most wonderful city, with the most wonderful people and the most wonderful work culture.

IT Saab—And what about the worst roads, the worst traffics, the worst houses that are so small and the worst work–life balance?

Bengal Rani—I think you are exaggerating. I have grown up in this city. I know what it is all about.

IT Saab (now in a super high pitched and offensive tone)—Bear in mind now, I will never ever shift to your city. Bear in mind from beforehand, if you have to stay with me, then you have to move away from this favourite city of yours which I dislike. Bear in mind, that I have no respect for your city and its people and its nightlife and its culture if that is what you call it. I have seen the best of the world. I like small cities. Let me tell you that you must bear in mind, that I will always live in tier two and tier three cities where there is space and work–life balance. That pigeon hole size home providing city of yours will never be my abode. So bear all this in mind. Do you understand?

Bengal Rani (on the verge of tears)—Got it. I need to leave. Bye.

IT Saab—Okay. Bye.

My friend consoles me and hurls as many abuses as he can remember on IT Saab. And then says—Bear in mind, never speak to this ass ever again.

I tell my parents that evening and they have understood. That is relief. I message IT Saab—Sorry not interested. He does not reply back. I think it was too hurting for his ego to do so.

So ends another day.

Another proposal.

And another The End.

Chapter 4

To Know the Man Ask His Bucket List

When I saw Telecom Raja's picture, I kind of looked at the mirror and heard it saying—you can do better. But there is this one frantic mood of the matrimonial mode where buying clothes and meeting prospective grooms becomes almost the same.

What is the harm in trying it? You can always return and say not interested. In many ways, this arrangement of making you meet your better half or perhaps that one person you would like to strike your strongest emotional chord with is rather a ruthless and emotionless procedure where often there are no marriages but an extremely high number of sensitive, invisible and bitter divorces.

Telecom Raja's grandfather was a hunter of his time. The hunter had finally settled for two wives and had taken God's command of multiply way too seriously. He had fourteen children of which many were settled in different parts of the first world and the few poor ones were still breeding and creating next generations in the third world.

One of those offsprings was Telecom Raja. A five feet five inches tall, MBA from the B school that had no other living its legacy, a job in the telecom sector that he was not really happy about and few articles that he had written some three years back which his father would rave about for the next three years and more.

So with this character sketch, we set ourselves on the starting line of the matrimonial race again. I was unsure by the very sight of him, but I reminded myself the standard five value education classroom lessons—a beautiful heart and a beautiful mind are more important and long lasting than a beautiful face.

Though I remember not being convinced about that line during my standard five days, I was always a bright student.

It was time to leave some of that brightness behind and speak to Telecom Raja.

I said my prayers for a decent non-Bengali accent and called. And my prayers were answered. He did not have a Bengali accent. That did not mean he had a British accent either.

Telecom Raja was a migrant to Mumbai. His toddler days and adolescence times had smelled the air of Ahmedabad.

Welcome to the Gujarati accent now.

Telecom Raja—Hi Bengal Rani. How's you?

Bengal Rani—I am very good. How have you been?

Telecom Raja—It is 7 pm. I have to stare at some more excel sheets for a while more and then I will run out of office.

Bengal Rani—Oh, that is an early day end is it?

Telecom Raja—No no. It is a very late day end. I push out by 5 pm.

Bengal Rani (surprised)—They let you do that? Really?

Telecom Raja—See my formula is very simple. I don't like working. I am okay with mediocre. I will never bother buying a car or a house in Mumbai. So I never take a job that will stretch to long working hours. My aims are not those things.

Bengal Rani (thinking how opposite he is)—But what about growth in life?

Telecom Raja—I am okay with this much. Don't think any more is needed. In fact let me tell you; I changed my job and rejected a promotion because I did not want to work beyond a certain number of hours.

Bengal Rani—Okay, so what do you do in your free time?

Telecom Raja—I travel. I watch plays. I think I will make a movie someday.

Bengal Rani (liking the fact that he at least has dreams and hobbies)—Movie making is a very creative thing. But it also needs the right money in place. Have you discussed finances yet?

Telecom Raja—When I have the plot in place I will. I have been working on it.

Bengal Rani—Oh for how long?

Telecom Raja—For the last four years. Don't get enough time you see.

Bengal Rani—But you just said that you do not work extended hours right?

Telecom Raja—Yes. But I watch plays. And then I have to sleep also.

Bengal Rani (understanding that this conversation is between an active woman and a lazy man)—I get your point. I am getting a call now. Can we speak some other time?

Telecom Raja—I suggest we meet instead.

Bengal Rani—Sure. Let me know the day in advance.

Telecom Raja—After two weeks will be good. You see I am travelling.

Bengal Rani—Okay. Where to?

Telecom Raja—Arunachal Pradesh. Ziro and the rest.

Bengal Rani—That sounds very nice. All the best. Have a safe journey.

Saying this much I breathe some peace. It is not that I have completely disliked Telecom Raja and also look forward to meeting him. However, sometimes a break is so necessary. These two weeks will give me a chance to relook at myself too and find out what looks like is in store for me. And for that I have to visit Kaya, the tarot card reader.

Kaya and I met some three years back. It was a chance meeting. Occult sciences interest me and the moment I got to know of Kaya's tarot skills I had to get a session done. It was perhaps the best future diving session that I encountered. Unlike the spooky, dark kohl eyed and heavy jewellery in garish robes women that normally take hold of your imagination when you think occult, Kaya was the very simple, elegant and soft looking healer of sorts. There was immediate connection and since then I have been a regular customer, which also led to one of the most beautiful friendships.

Just as per the plan, I was at Kaya's place at the designated time. Kaya looked at me rather carefully and noticed that I looked worried. She tried enquiring but often there is no real reason. So she smiled and I smiled back. Kaya had a very comforting smile.

Another wonderful act that Kaya did every time without fail is lighting a diya to her Little Lord Krishna. And I can guarantee you that you may be of any religion but her little Krishna would evoke only love in you.

Kaya—So what do we ask today?

Me—When will I find my ideal partner?

Kaya—Okay. Pull ten cards.

I did the practice one by one on intuition alone and picked ten of them and gave it to Kaya. As she turned them up one by one, I saw a pattern emerging, which she would explain soon.

Kaya—There are a lot of sword cards, which symbolize movement. Something is moving into your life. However, there is a devil card here and the position of it, I fear it will hinder the speed of things. I also see that the High Priestess is trying to tell us that what you have in your hands currently is not looking very reliable so be careful. There is something dark in it. Finally, I also see the Three of Cups and its placement symbolizes celebration, which means there is good news later this year but not immediately. Finally, the man who comes into your life is the maker or, let us say, the Merlin of his destiny. Thus, the Magician card.

Kaya had made her point and I had taken my notes. There was nothing very immediate, which means Telecom Raja would not materialize into anything for a long term. Not the best news, but it did not disappoint me to a great extent. After all, I had to revise my fifth standard value education classes to get myself to speak to him, which was a rather laborious task.

After the reading, Kaya and I sat for a while talking. I mentioned Telecom Raja to her and she said she could see there was a proposal but not promising enough to speak of. However, I must try and see. Miracles dwell where belief exists. One of her favourite lines.

Weeks passed rather quickly with a visit from my mother's elder brother's newly married son and his wife. I liked Rini immediately, mostly because she was an advocate of late marriages and had done one for herself. It fitted well in my current state of affairs.

So we travelled, ate at the finest places and finally when it was time for them to leave, they took a promise that I would visit them soon in Kolkata. I promised.

The morning of Week 2, Thursday, I saw Alisha stomping towards my cubicle. Normally, she doesn't look angry or vent. This was an abnormal anger, which often shows itself when either someone steals your hard earned diamond. Or if you meet an absolutely irksome guy through one of the matrimonial sites.

Knowing her life, I knew immediately it was the latter.

Alisha—I can't believe I meet such blokes

Bengal Rani—What happened Alisha? Drink tea. There is no problem in the world that a good cup of tea cannot solve.

Alisha—Sorry, I drink coffee only

Bengal Rani—Okay. There are also a lot of problems that a good cup of coffee can solve.

Alisha—If you shall keep throwing those lines at me, I will accept the fact that you are tired of me.

Alisha had her way of emotionally blackmailing, which was not particularly bad. In fact, sometimes, I found it funny. Anyways she did not wait for my reaction and continued talking.

Alisha—I spoke to a guy yesterday. This one stays in Toronto, Canada and is a doctor. He seemed okay when I saw his profile. A big nose, but okay.

Bengal Rani—If you are fine or even at an acceptable position with the way a man looks, trust me half the battle is won.

Alisha—Exactly, the motivation with which I moved forward. Then he said something so weird that I couldn't believe that man, and if I may say a well-qualified doctor in foreign land speaks such nonsense.

Bengal Rani—Like how bad?

Alisha—He says this. "Now that I have seen your photograph, I can imagine you to some extent. However, you have to help me imagine what you really are. So now, if I give you a scale as per which Kareena Kapoor is at nine and Konkana Sen Sharma is at five, where do you put yourself? How much would you rate yourself?"

Bengal Rani—He asked you to give yourself points? Marks?

Alisha—Yes from the sound of it he did. I was zapped. Couldn't believe that after ten photographs, he had asked me to do this. So I replied, "Your parameter and my parameter are very different". For me, Kareena could be five and Konkana nine. However, that doesn't amount to anything because with that question you gave me a perfect measure of your IQ which is a straight, hard ZERO. Don't ever call me again. I will complain if you do."

Bengal Rani—That is a lot. I am proud of you. You need a hug?

Alisha—You don't look like my mother, or like a man. No, some hilarious WhatsApp jokes will be good. I want to laugh.

I sent Alisha the one that I had and she went her way back to another colleague with the same story. I think talking was a fantastic therapy for most people. Especially women. Something that men should know about us. We women look to talk about problems. Solutions matter to us, but talking about our problems is just as important.

Anyways the meeting day arrived and that particular evening mom and dad were visiting some family friend. I had asked Telecom Raja to choose the venue which he conveniently avoided. Anyways I helped him and so the plan was locked.

I reached the venue well in time and waited. While I was looking through the menu, a blob of yellow entered the restaurant. Uneven with a wide torso and matchstick legs looking skinnier wrapped in tight jeans. Now, in a normal scenario, a fat uneven man entering a restaurant is perfectly fine. Trouble starts when the fat uneven man in yellow walks to your table and says—Hi. I am Telecom Raja.

It took me sometime to acknowledge the fact that I had been deceived to myself. This was the case of then and now in those quick weight reduction offer advertisements. In reverse mode though. The photograph in the site was of a much thinner man. Some of that had still been maintained. His legs were as thin as in the picture. But the proportion upwards had been vastly and hugely altered.

He sat in the chair opposite mine and we exchanged pleasantries finally. Then I noticed something. He was having trouble sitting straight and was stretching his legs leftwards to fit in. It was a rather sorry sight but I felt no pity. I was cheated for heaven sake.

Telecom Raja—The table is rather small.

Bengal Rani—It is still enough for two people. Don't you think?

Telecom Raja (changing the topic which is not fitting enough for his ears, just like the rest of him)—Have you been waiting for long?

Bengal Rani (thank God for the little shot of courtesy)—Not really. Just arrived few minutes back.

Telecom Raja—What would you like to drink?

Bengal Rani (glancing through the menu with little interest)—I think a Peach Iced Tea is good for me.

Telecom Raja—Why don't you try some cocktail instead?

Bengal Rani—No thank you. I am good.

Telecom Raja—Okay do you smoke?

Bengal Rani—No, I don't smoke.

Telecom Raja—You must try everything in life. You must give smoking a shot.

I didn't reply. Just, waited for him to order. The waiter arrives.

Telecom Raja—Get us one Peach Iced Tea and one White Maria.

Waiter—Sorry sir, there is nothing called White Maria on our menu. It is Black Maria.

Telecom Raja—Just tell your bartender, White Maria. He will understand, he knows me.

The waiter unwillingly takes the order and leaves. I remember that this man had mentioned that he had not been to this restaurant any time before.

Bengal Rani—Didn't you mention you have not been here earlier? How on earth does the bartender know you then?

Telecom Raja—Actually, I have been to this restaurant's other outlet in another suburb. There I had mentioned White Maria to the bartender. I am sure they must have spoken among themselves about it.

The fat left stretched man in yellow's confidence stuns me. He definitely had very high regards for himself, though the next few seconds did take away a bit of his steam.

The waiter came and informed that there was no White Maria and the bartender had no knowledge of it. Telecom Raja settled for its black twin instead. Black Maria.

Bengal Rani (thinking of a topic)—So how was the trip?

Telecom Raja—It was very nice. Ate great food. All sorts of animals.

I thought it was a joke until he started expressing his love for devouring all things that move. I took it with a pinch of salt and some acceptance as I too eat meat, but tried listening.

However, there was more to come. The horror didn't end there. Animals of every kind must run the moment they catch site of this man.

The more dangerous part.

The part which had a loud siren ringing in my head and screaming—Run and do not look back.

Telecom Raja—But what was best about this trip is that I was finally able to strike off one of the most important boxes in my bucket list.

Bengal Rani—Which is? (hoping that something more pleasant was to be spoken)

Telecom Raja (with tremendous passion)—I always, all throughout my life, wanted to see live animal sacrifice. I finally got to see it. A live bison sacrifice. Yes!

I could not get myself to react. My potential prospective groom's bucket list included live animal sacrifice. The next could be cannibalism.

I smiled and finished my drink in super speed.

Bengal Rani (to be sure)—You wanted to see animal sacrifice?

Telecom Raja—Yes, I did. For a very long time. You too must see it someday. The way the animal withers and runs. The way the sword cuts through. Oh pure sinister adventure!

Bengal Rani—I am better off without it. I like animals.

Telecom Raja—I do not hate them either. But a lot of them are better off inside my tummy.

And then Telecom Raja laughed loud. And I remembered The Haunted series.

In ten minutes I excused and left. I did not promise to call or stay in touch. Wasn't worth all the trouble.

So ended the day and my rendezvous with a man who was not too happy working, who cheated us over his present statistics, who encouraged me to smoke, and who loved the sight of a poor animal being sacrificed.

Rejecting him was not just life partner saving. It was life saving.

Chapter 5
He was Nice...However

I am a big fan of rom coms. And the moment Doctor Ji announced that he too was, I was elated. So, I would have company to watch all my favourite shows whenever time permitted. That was a good start.

Moreover, the good accent. Rather the normal accent. My ears were yearning to hear that. Another thumbs up for Doctor Ji.

Quite a fitness enthusiast though not overtly like one of those previous ones I told you of, Doctor Ji also believed in charity and donated a small part of what he made to one of the lesser known charitable institutions. His belief was that the smaller ones, which marketed themselves lesser, did more and grass-root level work. I agree to that. A small secret about Doctor Ji parents weren't aware of his act of kindness. He requested me to be quiet about it. I agreed to. So much modesty. Another sign of the prospective groom being a seriously great prospect.

So here I was. It was a week and I was speaking to a great heart specialist with a greater heart. Doctor Ji was everything right from the look of it. I wouldn't say I had an immediate crush on him or romanticized. But humanity sake, I couldn't ignore the niceness. And why would I? This was one of those, I was considering to get married to and spend the rest of my life with, waking up with. Every single day. It is actually that big.

Thursday evening, I was looking ahead to Doctor Ji's call. He of course was a busy man and I like people who keep themselves busy. It is a sign of them loving what they do. That's magnet for me.

The phone rings and I smile at it. After days, a product in the matrimonial market that I find normal, nice, intelligent and tolerable. All of these are so crucial.

Bengal Rani—Hi. How was the day?

Doctor Ji—Day isn't over yet. Still three hours to go easily.

Bengal Rani—You work a lot.

Doctor Ji—Don't you like that about people?

Bengal Rani—How do you know?

Doctor Ji—I could have said I guessed. But, however... you told me. I remember (laughter)

Bengal Rani (smiling that he has a sense of humour)—Aah, that way. Yes busy people are good people. I believe so.

Doctor Ji—All people are nice people. Busy people are more focused, nice people.

Bengal Rani—Actually, yes. Maybe what you are saying is more valid.

Doctor Ji—My dad told me this when I was growing. Think I took it from him.

Bengal Rani—You must be close to your father?

Doctor Ji—Yes very much. More than close I respect him. You see, he too was a doctor and a very successful one. Though he doesn't practice anymore, he lectures at some of the top medical colleges. I hope someday I can be closer to what he gained or let's say achieved. Yes, his word is very important to me.

Bengal Rani—Me too. I am close to my father.

Doctor Ji—You will like my dad. He believes in woman empowerment a lot. Yes, he is extremely health cautious but that's what work often does to you. Makes you a part of what it is.

Bengal Rani—Being health cautious isn't a bad thing

Doctor Ji—My dad does the right things. Most of the time, I actually follow his word.

Bengal Rani—Nice. So any plans for the weekend?

Doctor Ji—I think we are visiting your home, or vice versa?

Bengal Rani—Really? How come my father never told me!

Doctor Ji—Maybe my dad and yours haven't yet spoken. But my dad mentioned this to me. So mostly that is the way it could happen. Thought you must know.

Bengal Rani—Okay sure. Look forward.

Doctor Ji—Same here. Listen I got to go now. There is an emergency. You be good okay. And I shall see you soon.

Bengal Rani—Of course, you too be good and eat whenever you get some time. Goodnight.

Doctor Ji—Goodnight!

I am happy at the end of this talk today. Doctor Ji has principles for the right things. His respect for elders is remarkable. I appreciate that part of him more than anything else.

Because I love my father and mother. For me, they are the world.

I wanted to fly and I have wings. What mattered is, my parents let me fly. I have seen around. I know what happens to children when their parents obstruct their flight.

Dreams die. And life without dreams is one slumber mode in black. That's not nice.

That evening I called up Neel. In fact, we were due for dinner for a while. Neel is the 4 am friend that every girl needs, with or without marriage. He was married and I think must be a good husband. Though I hear how good or bad a spouse is, only his or her spouse can say. We just can guess. And our guesses are often not noteworthy.

What sugar is to ants, Burmese Khowsuey is to me. So when Neel announced the holy name, the priestess ran to get her chalice full and belly packed. Anyways every new proposal got mandatorily discussed with Neel. He has an excellent foresight and understanding of his own pack. Manhood.

Neel—So you like him do you?

Bengal Rani (placing the momos order first)—I think for a start yes. Though I am yet to see if he is exactly what I want.

Neel (the wisdom look quickly filling his face)—There is no exact darling. Okay, let's get straight. You can't get your man tailor made and customized.

Bengal Rani—Do you think I am asking for too much?

Neel—That is not the point. Point is the list. Why is there a list in the first place? Shouldn't it be natural?

Bengal Rani—There is no natural in the online matrimonial space.

Neel—Wasn't there in the beginning. Remember you were so excited once?

Bengal Rani—Yes. And with the way it happened I think I am convinced Perfect Marketer was not heterosexual.

Neel—Did he say he was?

Bengal Rani—Nobody says such things.

Neel—Did you see him cooing up to another man?

Bengal Rani—I saw him only twice.

Neel—Then, how did you decide?

Bengal Rani (raising my voice)—Do we have to talk about something that I wanted and did not happen? Do you have to bring this up now knowing well enough that it took me time to get over all of that? Now that I am hurt, are you happy?

I was louder than normal. And people were looking at us. Then I saw the commotion and scene I was creating, and gained composure. Though I was slow. And maybe it wasn't right on my part.

However, there was something in my past, which had not fallen exactly in place. And the memory of it had lingered a bit too far. Neel realized it wasn't the best example that night. And while dropping me back home, he promised to never speak of it.

Neel (not eating the momos that arrived, which he in normal days is the first to grab)—Relax…relax…relax.

We both waited for a minute or so, dug into the momos for the next few minutes, helped each other with the sauces to regain peace and then finally I spoke.

Bengal Rani—I am sorry. I am really sorry.

Neel—I understand. And my intention at any point was not to remind you of anything that was unpleasant. Two things that you should remember, why did you like anybody? That is the question. Did you like anybody you did for the right reasons? Every time you speak of any proposal, there is this common parameter that you border around.

Does he have a house in the city?

What is his salary range?

How does he look?

What is his position in the society?

I just have one thing to say. He might earn a crore a year. But how will it matter if he is the type who prefers an indoor life or has a mad mother. Remember that extremely promising guy you met whose mother had trouble in her head? She got fits every morning and all of that depression. He worked in one of the best FMCGs of the world and earned a bomb. Mrs Promising FMCG in return for years of mental disability handling? Was it worth the trade?

I looked at Neel and saw a lot of thoughts and wisdom that moment. Was I looking at people for the right things?

Neel—So custom made stems out of the same checklist that you are holding on to. A checklist is also fine. But are you holding the right checklist? I can tell you from my own life. I might make lesser money than many around me. But my wife and I are happier people. We take each day as it comes; we go for fantastic vacations, meet friends and party often, experiment with new and live a very complete and happy life. Isn't that more appealing to you? Or is it the tag, the salary, the house? That's the only point I am trying to make.

Bengal Rani (in complete agreement to whatever Neel spoke) I know Neel and I buy your point totally. But we are not talking checklists. I am speaking of a guy who looks like a potential partner.

Neel—Which is a very good thing. And I would be very happy for you if it works. I hope it does. All I am saying is for the real things and the more important things that need to be in a man you would want to see as a partner for life.

Bengal Rani (placing the khowsuey order)—We are meeting them on Saturday.

Neel—Good. So see how he is? His folks too if you are staying with them. Will they accept a working woman? And are they going to accept you lifestyle? Will you be able to adjust to their routine? All this matters.

I sighed. It looked so complicated. How could one who lives a particular life pattern and had been moulded in a certain way for years, break it and adjust to a new mould.

Neel (reading my mind)—Trust me. When it is right it is right. It will all fall in place then. Let it happen.

We smiled and changed the topic. Marriage wasn't our favourite topic anyways. There was so much in the world to look at and tell each other about. The food that we were eating, for example, was brilliant. And the dessert should we or shouldn't we question. Neel and I are diet conscious people. So we moved on.

And then came Saturday.

Doctor Ji's father had informed and contrary to normal ritual, we went to visit them. This was better. Why should my mom slog every time and fuss over what would go into the plate. Though the menu for any matrimonial sitting was set now. Chicken cutlets, paneer pakodas and a cup of tea with some fantastic dessert to end it. Showed we are a well to do family.

Doctor Ji's home was neat. Very neat. There was in every sense a hint of discipline in everything that had been allowed into the house. Bacteria and germs were far away from this household. The air smelled of some disinfectant my mom noted.

Just like the house, Doctor Ji and his parents were about eighty percent white. White t shirt and white pyjamas for the father and son duo and a slight hint of blue slippers. His mother was in a white saree with a very thin red border. So, we were the colourful lot in the home of whites. Which might not be such a bad thing. In most ways, we were the ones getting colour into their home.

We sat on the white sofa and while the regular hellos, nomoshkars, did you have trouble finding the house, smiles, more smiles, artificial smiles, more artificial smiles continued, their servant who resembled the quintessential filmy Ramu kaka in a white short sleeves vest and white dhoti (I think they took this colour protocol thing a bit too seriously) brought us some Marie biscuits and tea. Some colour at least.

As I bit the first Marie biscuit and made a mental note of how very hospitable my family is in terms of colour, food and drink versus these people, Doctor Ji's father broke into my thoughts with a rather unexpected question.

Doctor Ji's father—So child, do you take in vitamin pills?

Bengal Rani—I do. It is a good measure I hear.

Doctor Ji's father—Do you suffer from any ailments?

Bengal Rani—No nothing as of now.

Doctor Ji's Father—So when was the last time you sneezed?

I looked at my mom and dad for immediate help, who were taken aback with the question like me. However, my experience says that the older you get the better you become with your shock reaction capabilities. My folks look at me encouragingly. I understand that I need to cook up a believable answer now that is not scandalous or doubtful at the least.

Bengal Rani—Must be three months back I think.

Doctor Ji's father (noting the discomfort on our end)—Okay nice. I was just checking how healthy you are.

Bengal Rani—No problem uncle.

How healthy I am? Are they looking for a girl they want their son to marry or chicken for lunch? This was a rather awkward round.

Doctor Ji who I didn't mention looks better than in his snaps and has a good personality finally makes his entry in the conversation that is pretty one track at this moment.

Doctor Ji—You need to be healthy. After all, you are handling a very important role and doing some brilliant work.

I smile in return for the encouragement. Full marks to Doctor Ji on the Good Man Meter.

Doctor Ji's father—Oh yes, I believe that a woman is a complete woman when she is a working woman. Being independent is so important. These days death and mortality is so uncertain. One needs to be ready to face anything all the time.

Though I did not like the association of career with death, it is a good thing that the family patriarch is positive about my professional interests.

We speak more. About life in Mumbai, the city's roads, the politics of the country which is any Bengali's favourite topic after food and football, why is West Bengal not where it must be and the fact that it actually has the potential to be the greatest in the world (a belief that many Bengalis would kill for to keep alive) and finally about why there should be more Durga Poojas in Mumbai.

Through the conversation, Doctor Ji and I do not speak much...though I do notice that he is indeed very fond of his mother. Doctor Ji's mother hardly talks. She has in my view taken over the smiling business for the day and is simply happy doing that. The good thing is she did not ask me the can you sing, dance or cook questions, which says that this family might be more modern than the ones I met?

An hour passes by and my father signals that we must leave now, which is good because frankly I was beginning to look at my watch now. Doctor Ji's father talks a lot.

As we get up to leave and do the nomoshkars and hope for a positive gesture from their end, Doctor Ji's father decides to communicate once again.

Doctor Ji's father—So it all is good for now. However, you two need to speak more and tell us.

Doctor Ji and I smile at each other as the decision is rested upon us. The good thing is that there is enough time given for us to decide.

Doctor Ji's father (to my dad)—And I just wanted to tell you one last thing.

My father hopes to hear something encouraging from him. After all, they are a good family we have almost decided. A little colourless, but that is manageable.

Doctor Ji's father—We are not asking for it, but if you are giving, then let the house be in central Mumbai.

It took us sometime to understand what he was asking for. Dad, mom and I passed rather tense glances towards each other. I also looked at Doctor Ji, at the moment, who seemed visibly embarrassed and ashamed enough to not look back anymore.

Bengal Rani's father—Sorry, can you explain.

Doctor Ji's father—I simply said, that though we do not ask for it, if you wish to give it, then let the house be in central Mumbai.

The second request repetition that was curt makes the intentions very clear. Now, there is no confusion or doubt that we heard wrong.

My father looks at me and wonders what I am thinking. I am shocked and I wanted to reconsider my views on this family, the father and the son who had nothing to say whatsoever.

Bengal Rani—We don't wish to.

Doctor Ji's father—Excuse me? Did you say something?

Bengal Rani—You said if we wish to. We don't wish to.

Doctor Ji's father has a new expression on his face after my reply. I think we are at the end of this scene now with that dialogue delivered. But the story must conclude so I spoke.

Bengal Rani—Now that you understand our intentions, do you still want to consider this?

Doctor Ji's father—Well, give us time. We shall let you know.

Which clearly means that we shall make the same demand to other promising contenders and if at all, things do not work we shall come back to you with another smaller demand maybe this time.

My parents don't look angry. In fact, my mother who was quiet the whole time and normally gets very sad when things don't work in this front looks pretty normal and optimistic, which reaffirms my belief in my parents.

As we walked towards the door, I look at Doctor Ji one last time. He was still staring at the floor. I suddenly remembered his charitable actions that he had asked me to not speak about. Earlier, I thought it was modesty. Now, I knew the real reason.

As we head back, my mom holds my hand and convinces me that I did the right thing. My father too speaks his mind against Doctor Ji's father. I am feeling hurt too. It was a contradiction of my faith this time.

However, there are two facts that I encountered that day.

One, I was rejected.

Two, I was rejected not by a man. Or by a family.

But by a practice called dowry, which exists among the best of us.

Chapter 6

On My Time, or Goodbye

It had been two weeks USA Softwarewala and I were acquainted. I had been averse of moving out of my city to any other city. However, at this point, you must note that moving out of the country might not really be a bad idea.

So Mr USA Softwarewala who stayed in New York and worked as a software engineer in one of the firms and planned to do so for the next seven years of his life did not seem like a bad bet. I could go, bask in the glory of the American good life, make firang friends, upload as many pictures of the American cities I was soon to travel in my stay time there on Facebook, get likes and comments from friends and family who would secretly envy me…all in all live the American dream which many were dying to be a part of. This seemed like a good plan already.

We started skyping regularly. I think once in three days. Mr USA Softwarewala had a lot of questions and in a single day wanted to know almost everything. He was a little shorter than my preference and a bit overweight too, however he was also a successful Indian in America.

USA Softwarewala—You are beautiful.

Bengal Rani (blushing)—Thank you. I have heard that from you earlier.

USA Softwarewala—I still say you are beautiful. That picture of you in that saree! Will you wear the saree when you are in America?

Actually, I did not and still do not know how to wear a saree, but why admit and then there is always time to learn.

Bengal Rani—I hope you are not expecting that every day.

USA Softwarewala—No no, don't get me wrong. Of course, no one is asking every day. But occasions. Like Diwali or maybe Dasshera.

Bengal Rani—Oh why not. I like dressing traditional during festivals.

USA Softwarewala—Thank God. See you are so perfect and lovely. And beautiful.

Bengal Rani—You just said beautiful for about the third time now.

USA Softwarewala—You know I was so charmed with your pictures. It is like finding perfection.

Bengal Rani—We still haven't met yet. How do you know?

USA Softwarewala—I just know. One always knows. That's the thing about perfection.

Bengal Rani (happy feeling flattered)—Perfection is a far away thing. I need to work hard to get close to that, trust me.

USA Softwarewala—You are so modest. I think I like everything about you.

Bengal Rani—Well thank you. But isn't it time for you to sleep now?

USA Softwarewala—See you understand my time and work life so very well. That is such a caring gesture.

Bengal Rani—You actually told me to remember. And we are on different time zones.

USA Softwarewala—Right. Okay. So, now I have to go and grab some sleep. Though I wish we could speak longer. However, you know exactly what is right. So I shall follow what you say.

Bengal Rani—Okay then. Goodnight and sweet dreams to you. Sleep well.

USA Softwarewala—Goodnight to you too, though that fits my time zone better. Bye.

Every conversation had been just like this. USA Softwarewala in a matter of weeks was part of my social network and had put his like on practically everything I put up there. Every video chat started with praising how I was looking, how perfect was my dressing sense or how beautiful I was. He was head over heels in love and wanted me to know and reciprocate the same feelings. My mom who had been hearing the conversation outside my room though only by accident in her own words when I caught here, was the most excited living entity in the suburb of Andheri at that point of time.

One day, I got a message from USA Softwarewala that he could not wait any longer and would be coming to India in the next two weeks. I was thrilled, too. Finally, a face to face with the new candidate.

That evening when the Skype call happened he gave me his flight timings, spoke of a slight viral infection he was suffering from, almost cried with joy when I enquired in detail about his health as he was touched and finally mentioned how much he intended to spend time with me.

I told him that I would wait for his call and I looked forward to see him in person too just as much. I was excited this time. He seemed to be quite the right man. Moreover, his academic qualifications were very good and his future seemed a lot brighter than many I had known of. Life looked very promising with USA Softwarewala.

That evening when I met Neel for business purpose as he also provides consultancy services to the firm I work for, along with him came Nysa. Nysa was a sales professional in the company Neel worked for and keeping certain business requirements in mind, we would need both to work together on the current projects.

The magical part of the universal laws of life is that like attracts like. Often, when you are going through a certain situation in life and are wondering why me, you tend to meet many more who are more or less fighting the same battle. Once you get to know them, a comfort zone starts building around you and things seem not as bad as you thought they were. The pain is till finding those people.

Nysa and I just found each other that evening, courtesy Neel.

Post business talk, my matrimonial adventures started echoing in the air, thanks to Neel as those were his favourite gossip materials. To him the entire process is very amusing and he often finds humour in everything I say. That is one endearing quality of Neel that makes him a hit in the social circuit. Helping people lighten up is such a noble deed.

However today, apparently more than me was Nysa who needed his help. Twenty-eight-year-old Nysa was living her story on a certain matrimonial dot com, when she happened to meet a certain jerk who redefined what it means to be a jerk. After hearing her story, I am of the view that there should be a right to kill for safeguarding self-respect in this country.

Nysa—You will not believe what I encountered.

Neel—I know about it and I am still saying let's throw that creature in a bucket full of permanent black dye.

Bengal Rani—Permanent black dye? What is this about?

Neel—You really were of the opinion that you met the weirdest didn't you. Listen to her story. You will see weirdness in a whole new light.

I looked at Nysa. She did the "I assure you he is right" expression and started talking.

Nysa—So I met this guy, who earns less than me, looks okay and has a rich father. It was not really my idea but my father's.

Neel—Stop listening to your father now on!

Nysa—Okay that is not possible I have told you. However, coming back, this guy and I met after speaking roughly twice. I had suggested coffee but he was hell bent on a candle light dinner. During dinner, he asked me questions about my food preference, ordered exactly the opposite, asked about my hobbies, noted them down and said his were very different,asked my views on Salman Khan and then about my preference for pets, whether it was a dog or a cat. Ya!

Bengal Rani—Then?

Nysa—Then nothing really. He made me pay half the bill that day and we left.

Bengal Rani—A good guy never makes a girl pay the bill.

Nysa—And I paid for everything he wanted to eat, which was idli, curd rice and brinjal. I am allergic to brinjals so couldn't eat that, idli and curd rice are not part of my favourite palette. I tried asking him to get us some chinese or chaat instead but he kept the menu card to himself and made a comment on how unhealthy all of that was.

Neel—You should have got up and left.

Nysa—My father would have killed me had I done that.

It was clear that Nysa's father dominated her life in a big way. Parents can sometimes do such wrong things. They must learn from animals who just let go their offsprings.

Nysa—Anyways, the next day he called up and said that we must meet one more time. But during the day. I said sure weekend. But he insisted on anytime during the week. I said I have a job, but he was forceful. Well, I agreed unwillingly.

Neel—And this part you need to listen. You will feel like ripping the man apart.

What could a man who disliked chaat and chinese really do I wondered? He lived a spice less life anyways.

Nysa—So, we met on one of the weekdays last week. And when we did, he was waiting outside the cafeteria. He took my hand and I was thinking he would say something nice, while his eyes were fixed on my face. Then he looked at my hand very carefully out in the sun again and said, "I don't think this will work. You are nice and good. But I want my next generations to be very fair. So no point in going for coffee. You can go back to office. Sorry."

I looked at Neel and Nysa horrified. Could something of this kind really happen? Did such villains really exist in the modern India we live in? Though I had encountered an evil practice myself sometime back, however not just rejecting someone for colour but also being insensitive enough to spell it out to the person, and Nysa by the way has the looks of a dusky model with a great body and sharp features!

I could see how angry Nysa was while she was speaking of what she went through. And I felt the same anger building inside me. God, why do you let such people stay alive?

Then my phone rang and I was facing a whole new situation. USA Softwarewala had arrived two days back, which I knew about but was wondering why he did not call and wanted to meet us. Not me, but us. This was quite a contradiction of the conversations we had while he was in the United States. I did not like the sound of it. However at that moment, after Nysa's story I was mentally against the race of manhood. And I could know that about me. So I agreed and told my mom that I do not have any problem. She could say yes to the weekend plan.

I did not have USA Softwarewala's India number. So the scope of communication was nil. He had not been on Skype for a while now. Since I had nothing much to do than complain and wonder why, I decided to let go my worries and rather look ahead at what the weekend would bring. That evening when I reached home, dad looked worried.

Bengal Rani—What happened? You don't look normal.

Dad—Obviously. Your mom spoke to USA Softwarewala's mom.

Bengal Rani—So what is wrong with that. She did tell me about it and in fact took my permission before finalizing the meeting.

Dad (looking at me with the expression of "Picture abhi baaki hain mere dost")—Do you know where they are meeting us?

Bengal Rani (hoping it is not history repeating itself)—Say anything, but don't say hospital!

Dad—Okay, congratulations. It is not a hospital. But outside Dadar T.T. there is an old non-AC cheap thaali restaurant called Ganga Bhojanalaya. Sunday evening you, me and your mom have been invited there for a matrimonial chat with best compliments by USA Softwarewala's family.

I had seen Ganga Bhojanalaya. I do not know of the food, but it looked crammed and gloomy. On a not so normal, try to make ends meet day maybe one of my kind could visit the restaurant for thaali, however there were better thaali options in this city.

Ganga Bhojanalaya for a matrimonial family meet?

It was a rather peculiar choice. However, when the ball is not in your court, why beat the bat? So I consoled dad and said move on. Anyways I had some amazing new films in my pen drive to watch. Good cinema had the power to rectify anything.

My mom on her part was laughing about this particular choice of restaurant. She found it rather comical for a guy who had been spending such a major chunk of his life in the USA, could actually agree to meet in a place that was called Ganga Bhojanalaya. She laughed off the matter while we allowed Tarantino settle it for us.

So the week passed by consoling Nysa and deciding the menu for Alisha's house party which looked cancelled for now simply because half had other plans and the rest half were, well married! Ouch.

That apart the new brand campaign was the major time taker for the week.

So came the Sunday that we would fondly remember as The Ganga Bhojanalaya Debacle.

Mom—I think you must wear the white Indian suit.

Bengal Rani—What is wrong with black?

Mom—It is an unholy colour.

Bengal Rani—Nothing is unholy. It makes me look thin.

Mom (giving the "I give up, you are a bad daughter" look)—Do what you want.

Bengal Rani (trying to restore peace)—Can I wear the pink one?

Mom—The sleeves are too deep.

Bengal Rani—But that's normal for me. I wear deep sleeveless and short skirts, western dresses, etc. Why are we trying to show what I am really not?

Mom—After he likes you, show him what you really are. Today is the first meeting. Just follow the rules.

I think it is wise to not fight any further. If things don't really go right, then black and pink will be blamed my partners in crime and me the original villain, which I would feel really nasty about. So white it is for now.

The journey to Dadar T.T. is a rather uncomfortable one. We have a car. But it is not about the journey. The destination and the event that is to be executed there is concerning. My mom is still laughing over Ganga Bhojanalaya; I am actually wondering why USA Softwarewala has not chosen to speak to me after he reached Mumbai.

The rains have started visiting my city of dreams. As I looked out of the car, there was a greyish blue tinge to everything. It might rain soon or these could also be passing clouds. Whatever it is, rains are the most nostalgic affair of my city. It reminds of some forgotten love, a tear that hides in a concealed corner of your heart, a story that could never really start and everything incomplete. Magic.

Oh my God! No not this. As we finally entered the infamous Ganga Bhojanalaya (pun intended), a bigger revelation awaited us.

USA Softwarewala was sitting in between the seats, dressed in a dhoti kurta with his family. Who are —his mom, his dad, his two sisters, the two husbands of the two sisters, the kids of the sisters which are all in all four, his grandmother and the grandmother's attendant.

Talk about the great Indian family and blame it on Ekta Kapoor one more time. Ugh!

I am having a tough time controlling my anger. This is not funny. Not calling me after landing in Mumbai was not funny. Asking us to meet in a dingy place like Ganga Bhojanalaya is not funny. Getting an entire army of relatives to assess me, certainly NOT FUNNY written in caps on the black wall of nuisance in the darkest red.

We started talking. And yes, we means the families. There is absolutely no communication between USA Softwarewala and me. We just listen to what our families have to say, which is basically trying to find out what has not been typed so far on that matrimonial website.

His sisters checked me out as much as they could and I kept throwing artificial smiles about a kilo a minute. We Indians can be so much better in the acting business . It is such a day to day routine life thing for us.

After two hours of questionnaire solving, dosas, upmas, sheera and puri bhaaji gulping sessions which were drowned with cups of extra milk and too much sugar tea (which I hate and almost puke), the meeting was over. The pleasantries were exchanged, and we finally left for home.

Talk about relief.

Dad (while driving)—What do you think?

Mom (looking at me)—I don't know. What do you think?

Bengal Rani—Let's see. What do you think?

Dad—Are we all asking each other the same question?

Bengal Rani—Ya, because none of us have an answer I think.

Dad—True, let's see. But still, why Ganga Bhojanalaya? I don't get it.

Mom—And why that entire Ravana Sena together for a first meeting? I don't get it.

Bengal Rani—And why did he wear a dhoti kurta for heaven sake? I don't get it! At all.

Dad (since we all are left with no answers but a lot of questions)—Forget it. Let's wait and watch. Don't worry. Something or the other will work out.

Mom (giving the fake smile of hope when she knows things don't look right)—Yes, dad is right. And anyways, life is good.

The thing about family is they fight with you for your good. But when they see that good is not as good as it had promised to be, they hold your hand and say that good wasn't good enough. Better is on its way.

At least that is my family.

A week passed by and USA Softwarewala doesn't call. Nor do the members of his family and the extended family and we start forgetting about them.

But, there is silence before every storm. Didn't we already know that?

Like I mentioned the last time, calamity rings the bell when you expect it least. That afternoon while I was eating my lunch and reading the positivity steps to a good life article, and feeling that I am on the road to nirvana, positivity declared Exam Time!

Mom informed me of a rather strange communication that had arrived from USA Softwarewala's end. His mom's end rather.

They had liked me and are interested in marriage. However within the next two weeks on Friday 7.30 pm. Why the hurry, blame it on the stars of USA Softwarewala.

I need more time I announce and for once mom too agrees. Two weeks and no real meeting is too less. She and dad started speaking to the USA Softwarewala's parents about it and suggested anything six months later would be good.

They said that they will think over it and come back to us in a week's time with a possibly better solution. USA Softwarewala finally called me up and expressed his love for me once again and how perfect a match we were and how important it is for us to marry in two weeks, start life fresh and ensure that his grandmother who is the most important member of their family and suffering from some rare ailment fulfils her dream of getting a glimpse of her grandson's baby before entering heaven land.

I am not sure about this anymore and suggested that we decide about our lives first, let the dying die, and give each other more time as it is a matter of a lifetime.

USA Softwarewala in one of the phone conversations—But I love you, you and only you.

Bengal Rani—I know and I too kind of like you. But I think we both need to be very sure.

USA Softwarewala—But I am sure that you are the one for me.

Bengal Rani—Thank you but what is the harm in giving each other a little more time to understand each other. It is so much easier when we don't rush.

USA Softwarewala—But after marriage you have the entire time baby. Also, we can have our own babies.

Bengal Rani—See you are rushing again.

USA Softwarewala—Okay maybe the baby can wait. But I really want only you in my life. Let's do this.

Bengal Rani—You say you love me and I am the one for you. Can't you wait for the love of your life for some time? Is it that difficult for you?

USA Softwarewala—Thing is, I believe in horoscopes a lot. If I do not marry now, my growth and progress will be stunted for the next three years. This along with the fact that I love you and no one else. It is the right time for me.

I am stunned. A USA based extremely well educated software engineer is talking about the impact of kundali on his life and his extreme belief in it to the point that he is ready to be a part of a mistake if that's the verdict announced by the rulebook of astrology. What is the world coming to?

Again, blame it on Ekta Kapoor.

Bengal Rani (finally concluding with conviction)—Between love and superstition you have a choice. Let me know what you decide.

He doesn't answer for a whole thirty seconds. Then says a feeble Okay, I will call you day after tomorrow and let you know.

His call never comes.

But exactly two weeks later, on a date that looks familiar and was a part of our communication, I see his Facebook page relationship status updated.

Married.

This time I do not blame it on Ekta Kapoor.

Hypocrisy, yes maybe.

Chapter 7
The Curious Case of Purple

XYZ Agency! My motherland. With you as my teacher, I now have a solution to every problem under the sky. Even the India–Pakistan war.

And there were many more paragraphs full of similar gibberish.

That afternoon, my mom called me three times continuously though I disconnected the calls as I was part of an important meeting in my office. I instantly knew the reason behind this.

This was the 'finally found a good specimen' excitement.

In times like these, when you know that the pigeon will not stop fluttering its wings till you accept the message, always make sure you feebly pet the pigeon.

Through a subtle message.

Bengal Rani (whatsapping)—I will call you mom. I am engaged in some important work.

Mom—Okay, but call me soon.

I didn't answer any further. As of now, I have rented peace for the next two hours at least.

The meeting gets over half an hour later and I call up Arisa to prepare me for the next stranger that I will soon encounter. Arisa is one of my many friends who had received marital bliss but the bliss faded away slowly to the point that it is bogusly injected into the system for normalcy sake. Arisa, who was once an extremely independent and career-driven woman, is thirty-five today, works as a Vice President in a retail firm, and has about three months back accepted the fact that her husband is cheating on her for the last two years. And well, he will never be loyal. That's the bad news.

The good news according to her is that he will never bring his girlfriend home, and she may stay in the marriage bond. For children sake. Every time I speak to Arisa, I console her. I hear how much she hates this settlement. How much she was better off earlier when the ring wasn't around her finger. How there were no questions asked. Or no questions to ask. A time when the bags could be packed, and the unknown destination was all that mattered.

And how lucky I am to be single.

I fairly endorsed that idea. One of the most self-centred reasons of mine to speak to Arisa was that her complaints about her present day life and marriage make me feel rather great about my current state of affairs. I understand that this makes me a bad person. However, we are humans and we may have some negative thought which is valid. I think I made her feel good in the process as much as I could. So it is a win win for both of us.

Arisa—So you think your mom has again found someone?

Bengal Rani—No, two ways about that. She has some skills I tell you.

Arisa—Okay. Go give it a try. You are anyways at a better place than me.

Bengal Rani (getting a sense of the disturbed waters)—Are things not alright? As in, did anything happen?

Arisa—Yesterday, my friend saw them together, at a lounge in Powai. She called me and told me stuff. As in a lot of stuff. The one line that stayed with me was that he apparently had never looked happier. He was sticking to her like a leech and she too was quite addicted and wasn't taking her hands of him.

In a situation like this, where you are clueless about the entire story, consoling becomes a humungous task. I can tell her that, "hey don't worry. It is just a phase and he will come back. It's just physical attraction you know. Doesn't matter!" Point is matter it does. This vamp, for the lack of a better word has lasted in his life for two years. I have seen her picture, called her ugly and given her derogatory titles. But, the truth is that she is gorgeous. And she too doesn't seem like has any plans to leave him. I am sure she loves him too. And that is the most dangerous piece of information for Arisa. No, the woman is not after her man's money. She has plenty of her own. Actually she is after the man who is Arisa's man, better put the man who was Arisa's once upon a time.

Bengal Rani (on the lie to console track again)—It is temporary. You know, two years or maybe three or maybe even four. Someday it is bound to change. And honestly two, three or four, five years, all of this will not matter in front of those fifty years that you and he will have together.

Arisa (gaining confidence)—Do you think so? Will it fall in place?

Bengal Rani—Yes, it will. It always does.

Hope is the most potent saviour, and the most effective drug of our world. Every effective drug is also dangerous.

Arisa (now empowered)—See meet him. If he is good, we have the wedding bells ringing. If he is bad, you get to do some kicking.

We laugh and then talk about other important aspirations. There is so much more to life; you will realize when you speak to someone caught in a bad marriage. It is really the worst of the places to be in and thank God I am not living Arisa's life.

I called mom and I am right. She has actually bumped into a man she is sure I will love to marry. Sometimes, I feel it would be a very good idea to either record my conversations or put my mom in a nearby table when I do those meetings. The cover and the core are such contrasting elements I know now after meeting these ideal for marriage men.

Mom—He is your field man.

Bengal Rani—Okay, that is a great thing. But that's not what you wanted right?

Mom—I wanted you to have a kid by now. Does it happen as I want?

Bengal Rani (rolling her head)—Give me the details please.

Mom—I have messaged you his name and number. Check his LinkedIn profile too. Since his salary range is not mentioned, you might get an idea.

So, I finally read his LinkedIn profile. And his patriotism for the agency that taught him everything from scratch perhaps and trained him well enough to well solve what governments across the world had failed to do.

Such was the entry of Mr Brand Kalakaar in my life. One thing was sure from what I understood. He loved to write and would one day surely dabble in the author's world. Second, he had secrets.

A man who talks too much, hides too much.

However, still, because marriage is priority and I have to give things a try and like Arisa said I will either have bells ringing or put myself together to deliver some kicking, I decided to call Brand Kalakaar who is working at the moment with one of the top PR firms of this country.

But not right now. Right now there are greater things to do. An event to attend, promote and speak in favour of my organization's latest work, talk about the campaign we are planning, pick some worthwhile contacts, hard sell my CV for a better place in the market, notice some men, make a pass and give them a not available signal in case they are not serious, and the we must meet signal if any of them look genuine and promising, eat great food, bitch about competition and then get home as the city's traffic tends to drop later in the night.

That is my life in short. I like networking and being a part of engaging conversations. My job has given me the privilege to meet some very influential and knowledgeable people. This is the reason why my sense of communication is evolved and elated to quite an extent.

And also why a promising groom with a worthy CV fails to impress me if he cannot hold a conversation and speak better than me.

Next morning, I am pretty excited. The hot yoga classes I enrolled for have finally started. Recently, I had watched Miranda Kerr's way to a great body through yoga videos. And I so loved what I saw that I knew, I had to do this.

We Indians love everything Indian, the moment the West loves it. How cheap of us. Anyways, we are like that only.

It is one of the best exercise sessions I have encountered in my life. I have experimented with many forms of exercises ranging from pilates to belly dancing to cardio or zumba or even pole dancing which was a fashionable workout regime two years back from now. But it faded and it was meant to. Very few exercise regimes really stand the forever test of time. Hot Yoga is one of those few.

After the many asanas, the final shavasana and meditation which contrary to public opinion is not about concentrating on God or thinking of the powers of the universe. Thoughtlessness and blankness of the mind is meditation. That is perhaps the most apt and simplest definition. And I did all of that in a room which had its temperature raised with a heater; one of the most vital aspects of hot yoga.

So after that power dose this morning and a heavy breakfast of potato tikki sandwich, I decided that today is a new chapter of my life. And I shall dedicate a small paragraph of it to Mr Brand Kalakaar.

Midday I dialled the number, expecting if nothing then at least a normal man.

A female voice—Heleyo (with a loaded Brit accent)

I might have dialled the wrong number. Why else would a girl pick? Still I better ask as colleagues can pick calls often.

Bengal Rani—Sorry I need to speak to Brand Kalakaar. Maybe I dialled the wrong number.

The voice—This is the right number. Who is calling if I may have the pleasure to know?

Oh my God! The female voice doesn't suddenly sound hundred per cent female with that second line. There is a tinge of masculine in it. Maybe the ratio of female versus male in that vocal sound is seventy by thirty or eighty by twenty, which brings us to the conclusion that Mr Brand Kalakaar has the voice of a Kalakaarini.

Bengal Rani—I received your number from my mother regarding an online matrimony proposal.

Brand Kalakaar—Oh my God! Ms Bengal Rani, is it not you?

Bengal Rani (still suspicious if it's a guy or a girl)—Yes, it is me.

Brand Kalakaar—How are you my friend? Such a good thing we speak. I am feeling privileged.

Gosh, he talks like a duchess.

Bengal Rani—I am doing very well. Thought it would be nice if we connected.

Brand Kalakaar (sounding very excited)—Okay then I have a brilliant idea. Let's not get into this know thy over the phone mode at all. Let's meet. Like normal people. Have some coffee and spend some quality time together. Don't you think that will be a much prettier idea?

Pretty! Do guys use those words for anything except women?

Bengal Rani (beginning to see that something is just not in the right place)—Okay, when do you suggest we meet?

Brand Kalakaar—Today is the best day of the week Madame. You know why? Today is Leonardo Da Vinci's birthday. I love that man. Let's raise a coffee toast to Leonardo this evening.

Bengal Rani (very perplexed at the speed at which things are moving but still willing to know ring or kick as soon as possible)—Okay will do. The coffee shop in Goregaon, Oberoi Mall.

Brand Kalakaar—See you love. Bye!

Bengal Rani— Yes, Bye.

I disconnected the call and wondered what that really was. This is perhaps the funniest I have interacted with and I am really not thinking whether I will like him or not or vice versa. I am in mood for a comedy show for now and this well, looks promising.

I informed my mom and she suggested to come home and dress up. But I cook up the regular cock bull story.

I mentioned the ring versus kick debate . I already know this is not the match I intend to meet. So, entertainment is my only motto for this evening.

And today evening 6.30 pm, the show begins.

Brand Kalakaar is late by fifteen minutes, though he was courteous enough to call and apologise. The apology just like his LinkedIn profile was too wordy and exaggerated.

I looked around and saw a lot of college romance blooming around me. No matter the shelf life, this young immature romance is perhaps the most real one. It is genuine at least. Whether permanent or temporary. But real.

Click click. A floral hand clicks its fingers and brings me back to reality and I further looked up to see the one the floral hand belongs to. Mr Brand Kalakaar is standing right in front of my table in full bloom in his floral florescent green tight shirt with sharp skin tight jeans that cover up and in my view suffocate his bottoms. He is smiling so wide that it is becoming absolutely impossible for me to not laugh.

But laugh I must not. Can't hurt our dear…well…man's feelings.

We started with a hug and cheek to cheek muaah.

Brand Kalakaar—I am so glad you are here. Can't believe me meet darling.

The last time I met Mrs Nanny, my fifth standard piano teacher, she said the same line with the same gestures.

Bengal Rani (ensuring that there is politeness at least)—The pleasure is mine.

Brand Kalakaar—So before we start, let's fill our tummies. What do you say to that?

Oh God! Every line is more feminine.

Bengal Rani—I will have some coffee. That's all.

Brand Kalakaar—Hey don't worry. It is the first week of the month. Pockets are loaded!

I looked at him unsure and then he laughs like an orangutan got a whole walnut stuck in his throat.

Brand Kalakaar—So we shall order, the lasagna with chicken and since I am allergic to fish, can a low calorie salad sandwich do?

Bengal Rani—Allergy you mean?

Brand Kalakaar—Acne baby. Gives me sleepless nights.

Low calorie diet conscious and petrified of acne. I asked for entertainment didn't I?

Bengal Rani (not ready to ask for anything more)—Okay, whatever you choose.

Brand Kalakaar—Are you sure? You really think this is also what you want? You can tell me, I will understand.

Bengal Rani—That is really sweet of you. But I think I shall be good with this.

Brand Kalakaar—Alrighty. So we order. And then we talk.

He calls the waiter in a rather obscure manner. With a wink. Anyways the orders are given.

Brand Kalakaar—So let us first speak of the weaknesses, because we have plenty. Oh can you just stand my umbrella next to that wall behind you?

Bengal Rani—Sure. Where is it?

The next two minutes I took time to recover. His umbrella was pink in colour with blue polka dots. Pink is for girl. Blue is for boy. His baritone, sexual status and umbrella seem to all be in the same female versus male ratio. Eighty by twenty.

Bengal Rani—That is a rather, pretty umbrella.

Brand Kalakaar—Don't you agree? I don't know what it is with people. They don't seem to quite like it or agree with the umbrella.

I mentally screamed, they don't agree with the one who is carrying the umbrella. The umbrella is all fine and good.

Brand Kalakaar—So let's play a game. Let me know you with a few quick choices. Ready?

I am not sure if I am really ready or whatever. Mentally, I am laughing at this floral wonder sitting in front of me.

Bengal Rani—Okay, ready.

Brand Kalakaar (excited by the sound of it)—Okay, so first question. Mozart or Beethoven?

Bengal Rani—Mozart (because I never heard Beethoven and all of India has heard Mozart thanks to Titan)

Brand Kalakaar—Sachin or Dhoni?

Bengal Rani—Sachin.

Brand Kalakaar—Why not Dhoni?

Bengal Rani—I like Sachin.

Brand Kalakaar—I think Dhoni is pretty hot you know (there is this hint of mischief in his eyes.)

Brand Kalakaar—Anyways, next question. Pink or Blue?

I bet he cannot answer this himself.

Bengal Rani—Purple (saying this I laughed loudly. This could be his favourite colour, maybe).

As I continued giggling and marvelling at my own words, I see Brand Kalakaar all serious and red faced. Oops!

Bengal Rani (back to seriousness)—Did I say something wrong?

Brand Kalakaar—You are just like the crowd. I thought you were special. You are a Bengali after all!

I liked the special part though I didn't recognize what Bengal had to do with it.

Bengal Rani—See I did not mean to offend you. I just said you know, said something that I found amusing to myself.

Brand Kalakaar—That is the deal with the world. Amusing to oneself. Have you ever realized how the man you all victimize feels? Creativity will have a hint of feminine to it. But that still keeps me a man. Why do you all make such nasty comments at me? Am I not talented? Am I not a golden heart? Am I not human?

He was actually serious. Brand Kalakaar was in full knowing of what the world thought of him, which was sad. But necessary for him.

Brand Kalakaar—One day, I complimented a guy in my office for his new jacket. Do you know what he said to me? Take a guess.

I didn't have one but still…

Bengal Rani—Thank you?

Brand Kalakaar—No, it is a world where cruelty rules and Shakespeare is doomed. He replied, "Well, I am not removing it and giving you a good time if that's what you are trying for. I am not what you think."

So I was now relieved that my judgment was right and it wasn't just me. His people had the same views about him.

Brand Kalakaar—But I am a man of Tagore's land. I replied, "You small brain. I too am not what you think. Bad news for you."

Bengal Rani—Oh then things must have got better right since he and people in your office got to know.

Brand Kalakaar—God is not always kind my dear. The next day, I saw a caricature poster of me gone viral. It had me draped in a saree and screaming. The caption was 'Behen Ka Gussa!'

Honestly, I felt bad for him that moment. This was not the way one treats anybody. People's sexual orientation or for that matter their style no matter how strange, is their personal choice. Choose to not speak to him or her, but mockery is not acceptable.

Bengal Rani—That sounds terrible. Did you complain?
Brand Kalakaar—That ruins my chances to make friends.

Bengal Rani—Not really. That in fact sends a signal that this better stop. You are not ready to allow people to damage your self-respect. If you think keeping quiet will help you, trust me you are only inviting more trouble.

He looked at me and heard me very intently. And then, he requested me to help him create an email for his organization's management, which I happily agreed to do.

As I typed the mail, I also got to understand that apart from the obvious female attributes, Brand Kalakaar was also an exceptionally intelligent and creative individual with more understanding of brands, world politics and cultures than me. He was in fact a walking encyclopedia on Egyptian history and we spoke for a long time that evening.

He was not a homosexual, he admitted. However, Brand Kalakaar's dream woman was very unlike me. He wanted to be with a very athletic, strong, practical and no nonsense woman with short hair. He was sure enough to make a note of the woman's hair length.

Brand Kalakaar—We often try to find in others what we lack. I am not the macho Rambo that woman prefer. I hope to have my partner filling that empty space and the gap perhaps. No, I don't want a masculine partner. But I want a strong woman. Looks strong is strong. That kind.

I listened to him and realized that he was able to do what I wasn't. Understand what he really wanted. I still struggle on that. I was truly happy meeting Brand Kalakaar.

Finally, the first draft of the letter was ready and it read like this.

Dear Sir,

I would like to notify that I am one of the employees of your reputed advertising agency working as an account director for some of the top financial clients that take services of our agency. My tenure here has been seven months and I have a total experience of six years in this field.

Today, I am writing to you to not discuss salaries or late work timings. Those are very small and besides I love the work I do. However, the question of respect. My colleagues have repeatedly targeted me because I come across as a man with different sexual preference than what the world calls normal. Since I am not, this is unfair. And if I was, then too this is unfair. A person's sexual preference is personal choice and no one has the right to mock it or condemn it or lastly question it. The comments and ridiculous acts by my colleagues have reached an unbearable limit and I am attaching a poster that was designed and made viral when I objected to it. Kindly have a look at it.

I understand that in your busy schedule it would be very difficult to give this incident much time. However, I would be grateful if you did.

Warm Regards,
Brand Kalakaar

Brand Kalakaar true to his style had tears in his eyes while reading it. He sent the mail immediately.

Brand Kalakaar—You are an angel you know that.

Bengal Rani—The angel hasn't found her hero yet.

Brand Kalakaar—Oh come on. You will find and not one, many! I know it darling. I have seen more of this world.

We laughed. The man who I was mind-mocking was now telling me how awesome I was. It felt good.

Few days passed and Brand Kalakaar and I started speaking very regularly, though I informed family that this was not happening. Broke mom's heart, but there was no way I could have avoided really.

A week later, Brand Kalakaar called me. He was so happy that I could actually picture him dance like a dolphin.

Brand Kalakaar—You are the greatest and the best I met!

Bengal Rani—What happened? You sound like you got the moon.

Brand Kalakaar—I did darling. Guess what happened. The CEO called me to his cabin today and I was sweating. Like God knows that that letter has done. Then he said,

"I apologise for what this company has done to you. It is my fault too and I take blame. Since I can't make things right immediately, I have a suggestion. Will you take up the position of Senior Account Director for all our FMCG brands in Singapore?"

Bengal Rani (almost falling off the chair)—What are you saying? Really! Like really really really!

Brand Kalakaar—I jumped I tell you. This is the best thing that happened in my life ever. Imagine Singapore and such an awesome position. All because I chose to respect myself.

Bengal Rani (feeling good)—Always choose respect. It is perhaps more important than any other element in this world.

Brand Kalakaar—You are awesome. I can't ever forget that. You have given me this. Thank you…thank you… thank you!

Bengal Rani—Stop thanking me. I just reminded you about who you really are.

Brand Kalakaar—Still thank you! You are seriously so so so good.

Bengal Rani (now wearing the mischief hat)—Okay that doesn't mean I don't get my treat.

We both laughed this time. Loudly and genuinely. I was really happy for him.

We decided to meet before he left and yes we did. It was really great the way it happened and somewhere it was a lesson for me. Maybe I underestimated him and people generally a bit too soon. I had something to work on which means.

So this time, like previous times, I did not find a husband.

But this time, unlike previous times, I found a friend. For a lifetime.

Chapter 8
A Weekend of Womanhood

Alisha—Do you know there are agencies these days to find out how authentic these profiles are?

Bengal Rani—Don't tell me. You can't be serious on this.

Alisha—I am telling you. I just got the card of one.

Saying this. Alisha pulled out the visiting card of RevealPartner detective agency out of her pocket and placed it in front of me. The tagline of this agency was "Uncovering your partner's every move."

India is an economy of jugaad. There is actually enough of everything in India beginning from its population which continues to tear the ceiling in spite of the Government investing heavily on the family planning propaganda. The by-product of this extreme number of livelihoods is availability of services of every nature.

Now, since we have matrimonial sites booming in our country and crores of profiles hitting and listing into it every day, there is a possibility of fake profiles; hence, it is a good idea to contact agencies to investigate and find out if your potential partner is really as worthy as he claims to be. That's what RevealPartner is all about. If you like a man on an online matrimonial site, you may meet him and his family, and if things look good or very good, then you can double check with RevealPartner. They are the last mile attendants.

Is there any other element that makes detective agencies like RevealPartner establish in a country like ours?

Well, we Indians are propagators of the One Life One Marriage theory. Moreover, it doesn't hurt to be safe.

Alisha—My friend used that service. That guy who she was about to marry, the one who claimed to be a doctor, was actually a pharmacy salesman.

Bengal Rani (taken aback)—What? Like really? Salesman against a doctor?

Alisha—I was equally shocked in the beginning when she told me about it. But then the pieces of the puzzle came together and a more reliable picture emerged. His work involved meeting only doctors, and over years he had gained a complete know how about their life, schedule, habits; practically everything. You won't believe that for the third round which involved meeting the guy's parents, he actually raised a set of fake parents. Thankfully, this friend's sister's friend's nephew is a doctor who got suspicious when he saw the guy's photograph. This salesman had visited him for one of the drugs his company was probably promoting. That's how things first came into notice. However, the thug was quite sharp and she was just not ready to believe that she was being taken for a ride. So her parents and bless them because it was their idea, hired this detective agency and in seven odd days, the sirens blew. He was a sham.

Sitting in a metropolis and knowing mostly good and genuine people for most of your life, the comfortable safety fence that I was mostly surrounded by never really allowed me to think that such stories were possible in the realms of reality. All such incidences in my head thrived in perhaps the suspense and mystery section novel collection of my library. That was where they belonged.

That evening, as I told my mom about this incident that Alisha had narrated to me, she did not express astonishment over it at all. According to her, human character is capable of deception. Deceiving and being deceived both. However, she quickly saved the details of the agency in her mobile and hoped we would need to contact them soon. In her view, the moment I like a guy, she and dad would do a thorough investigation done of him, his family and his relatives. Technically going to RevealPartner equals to me saying yes for a guy. That was the line she was dying to hear.

My mom was lucky in matters of heart. She had found love early in life. She and my dad had been married for three decades now, and it was if not a marriage of two perfect people, it was a marriage of two people perfect for each other.

I also feel in her times, people were more serious about love and viewed it as a life-long commitment. Needs were simpler, people worked hard and the rulebook of right and wrong had either a darker handwriting and bigger font or people had a better eyesight.

Mom—By the way, there are two families that have reached out to us.

Bengal Rani—Two?

Mom—You should be happy. You are in demand.

Bengal Rani—Are you sure you are not beginning to make a hobby out of this and doing it just for me?

Mom—It has been more than a year Missy, that I have tried making a Mrs out of you. If it was anything of a hobby ever, then it is not anymore. It is labour now! What will you do when your cousins start announcing marriages? They are younger. Just think about it.

Indians never lose their cool over their own problems not solved. We lose our cool when others solve the same problems which are giving us sleepless nights, before us.

Anyways moving on, she gave me a brief description of the two new candidates. One was heading the supply chain department in a multinational company. The other was a Chartered Accountant. So MNC Supplyman and CAchand were the latest butterflies to enter and get trapped in my mom's matrimony net. I would now assess them to know if these were serious butterflies or beautified moths.

I decided to do things differently this time. One call and then a straight meeting seemed to be a much better way of immediately deriving results. So when I called MNC Supplyman and asked him for a meeting the coming Sunday and he agreed, the job seemed half done.

CAchand was a different sort of a butterfly though very particular about timing. He mentioned that he had studied astrology for years and in his opinion every great step of life should be taken in the right time. Basically, he would check if all the stars approved the Saturday 6 pm meeting and get back to me. His conduct did set the alarm bell ringing in my head; however, I silenced it and told myself—hang on, just a fun hobby maybe.

In the meantime, I anyways had to make arrangements for two big events in Bangalore and Delhi that the organization

I worked for was participating in and simultaneously had a whitepaper to finish which thankfully took most of my time. Hence, the week passed by without allowing me to think much.

However when Friday came and the morning brought tense stares from my mom, which clearly translated to—you better meet the boys, I decided that it is the time to act. Matrimonial meetings after a point are simply a check in the box and not actions involving enthusiasm or nail biting excitement, until and unless the candidate is really good. That hadn't happened for a while.

Anyways, I called up CAchand to find out if the sun, moon and stars were in my favour this time. Luckily they were, with a slight change. We had to see each other at six minutes prior to six. Okay, this was not just a fun hobby.

When Neel and Kaushal heard about CAchand, they were both very clear that they wanted a live demonstration of this man. So a plan was hatched to have them around when I met him.

Bengal Rani—Are you serious? This is risky.

Kaushal—You are meeting a guy who asked you to meet him at six to six. Because he thinks it is safe or auspicious or whatever. This is risky!

Neel (giggling)—My worry is different and of long term. How will you have kids with a guy so impeccable about timing?

Kaushal and Neel take immense pleasure in pulling my leg over everything under the sun. And they are hell bent on seeing what a matrimonial meeting is like. Neel already has someone in his life and Kaushal is done with having too many someones in his life. A matrimonial meeting hence looks like a highly unlikely phenomenon for both my friends.

Saturday finally dawns in my life and Neel picks me up. Kaushal will join us at San Churros, Khar, which is the meeting venue for the day.

Bengal Rani—You guys be sober please.

Neel—What does that mean?

Bengal Rani—Don't do anything stupid.

Neel—Can we laugh? If we have to.

Bengal Rani—Facing the other side. To the wall. Or I shall start laughing and that will be embarrassing.

Neel—By the way you are looking good. So well dressed to meet a guy who asks you to meet him at six minutes to six because it is auspicious? Really!

There is no end to hilarity and reminding me about CAchand's astrology obsession.

Anyways when we reach, I enter first and take a place and Neel comes in later and takes a place opposite mine. That way he and Kaushal, who joins him in a while, can enjoy the show in full view.

So the scene is set and Mr CAchand can arrive any moment. It is showtime anytime now.

And like lightning strikes, CAchand arrives. At six minutes to six. Wearing a shiny turquoise blue kurta and black lose pants. His hair is oiled and he smells of, if I am not wrong, mustard. A sharp acrid smell that makes me want to run. He has a tikka on his head and a rudraksha rosary around his neck.

Haven't I seen enough tragedy dear God? I wonder.

CAchand (walking towards me)—You must be Bengal Rani. Why are you wearing green today?

Bengal Rani (pretty uncertain on the basis of that question)—What is wrong with green? I like the colour.

CAchand—That way, I like Hrishikesh more than Mumbai. But destiny and my karmabhoomi (land of duty) are meant to be in this city. Hence I stay here, wear shirt and pant and go to work. Green is not the colour for Saturday.

Bengal Rani—Are there any colours for Saturday?

CAchand—There are colours for every day. But Saturday's black is the most crucial. You see, Shani's colour is black.

Bengal Rani—(confused)—Who is Shani?

CAchand (giving the look of can't believe you just said that)—Shanidev. The God. The planet. The son of the Sun.

Bengal Rani (even more confused)—Wait a minute. Shani is God, planet or son?

CAchand (dejected)—Bengal Rani, you have learnt nothing. But okay it is a good point to start our conversation on. I will explain the greatness of Shanidev to you today, while we both drink black coffee.

Bengal Rani—I don't like black coffee.

CAchand—Dear, I told you, black is the colour of Saturday. You must wear black, eat black and feel black. Just do as I say. For your own good.

I had made a mistake by asking him questions. The next one hour, CAchand dedicated to Shanidev, who I have no hard feelings against, but was forced to listen about. Who is Shani, why is he what he is, is he God, demi god or planet. Why does he like black, who are his best friends and enemies, his partiality to mustard which also explains CAchand's smelly pungent hair for the day and of course how strictly the rules must be followed to ensure that Shanidev likes you.

The rate at which CAchand was talking about his complete devotion to the rulebook of Saturday Shanidev conduct, I was convinced that he could call eating a crow valid since it was black and a Saturday.

On the table opposite me, I could witness the amusement that Neel and Kaushal were deriving. Kaushal who is also a wonderful artist was busy sketching this character I was entertaining at the moment. Neel was taking Shanidev notes and cheering me with the uncanny actions to continue speaking to him further.

CAchand—So now since you have understood the benefits of the way I lead my life, you should know one more thing.

Bengal Rani—Which is?

CAchand—I will not marry you till the time my guruji gives you a go ahead. I know this piece of information will hurt you, but I have the greatest faith in my guruji.

Well, I was not hurt at all, but his stupidity was mildly entertaining for me too. So I continued to listen.

CAchand—You see, there was a girl before you too, who my parents asked me to meet and I liked her. She was also a follower of Shanidev and astrology rules. But my guruji rejected her.

Bengal Rani—So you did not marry her because your guruji said no?

CAchand—Yes I did not. It was difficult because my parents were very much in favour of the girl. She was not bad to look at and she earned well, and she came from a very good family. But guruji said no. Then no.

Bengal Rani—You never reasoned it out with your guruji?

CAchand—You never question guruji. You accept what he tells you to do.

Bengal Rani—Okay, I get it.

CAchand—So since I am as honest as I am, I think it is best for me to tell you the whole truth. Since my parents were not ready to agree to my decision, one night before the marriage I ran away.

Did he just say he ran away a night before his marriage? Neel and Kaushal stopped doing whatever they were doing and glared at him with their mouths wide open.

CAchand—First train to Indore to the ashram. I ran away.

Bengal Rani (still trying to make sense of the conversation that is going on)—Then?

CAchand—Then nothing. Stayed there in my guruji's Indore ashram for fifteen days and waited for things to cool down.

What is this man…and what is this guruji!

CAchand—Then my guruji and I hatched a plan. Coming back was not easy as there would be tension and questions. So we decided to take a separate route. Saturday morning at seven minutes to nine my parents got a call. A gruff voice announced that I was kidnapped.

Pin drop silence. I don't have it in me to ask him any further questions. He may continue.

CAchand—A ransom money of five lakhs was demanded.

Bengal Rani—And they gave it?

CAchand—I am their only son. And my father is loaded.

Bengal Rani (In total disapproval)—That is very bad what you did. It is unethical.

CAchand—No, I did not keep that money. My guruji's ashram is in dire need of money. So I donated all the money to his ashram.

Bengal Rani—Is he staying in Indore?

CAchand—No, in Mumbai. He has ashrams in Indore, Chennai, Amritsar, Kolkata and Ahmedabad.

Bengal Rani—Didn't you just mention he is poor?

CAchand—Yes, he is. He is setting his next ashram in New York and doesn't have enough resources. That means he is poor.

Bengal Rani—But once you came back, didn't your parents try to marry you off to that girl?

CAchand (giving a very devilish grin that I hated immediately)—My darling, this is India. A marriage called off is the worst nightmare for any girl. So when I disappeared, her parents married her off to the very next guy who agreed. You see, destiny had different plans for her. Poor thing, suffered. But Shanidev was merciful to me.

I was fuming by then. If there is anything that irks me more than a bad headache is a man who looks down upon womanhood. And today was my day of demonstrating. Luckily the two men in the next table were in full agreement with my anger.

I got up with the black coffee which was somewhat hot in my hands. Now it was real showtime.

CAchand—What happened? Twelve minutes to eight is the best time for us to say goodbye.

Bengal Rani—Look at your watch.

CAchand—Why?

Bengal Rani (blunt)—What is the time?

CAchand (beginning to get nervous) —It is five minutes to seven.

Bengal Rani—Perfect. Shanidev just whispered into my right ear that five minutes to seven is the best time to teach a moron a lesson. With a not so hot cup of black coffee.

And I then threw the entire cup of black coffee on his face in one go.

The restaurant stopped functioning for a moment. There weren't enough people around to see what had happened, but the few who were noticed. Neel and Kaushal clapped.

CAchand was in a state of shock.

Bengal Rani—This is for spoiling a girl's life and not being sorry for it. Will you ask your guruji whether I am good for you? I know your guruji by now as I have seen his Facebook fan page flashing on your profile. I will with the help of my journalist friends get a story done on the ugly business of babas. Just wait and curse your stars. No amount of black and mustard can really save you.

Saying this much, the offended me marched out. I didn't wait to see what happened of him or if he was coming with any weapons behind me. Honestly, I did not care. That day, I knew I had done the right thing.

And I am never sorry for the right things I do.

Neel and Kaushal both tried contacting me, but I messaged back that I am fine and kept my phone aside. I needed to be with my God to get back to normal.

I am not a believer of horoscopes and stars. But I believe in the power and goodness of God. And thank God he never fails me.

Honestly, I was not ready for the Sunday that was about to come to meet yet another man. I cried through the night.

It is not easy being where I am, especially if you care about the impact of your life and status on the people who matter most to you. My single status affects me. But it affects my parents too and often the way our Indian society is, it leaves them in a very uncomfortable position. There are questions by acquaintances and far off relatives who meet them probably decades later and out of the three most probable questions they would ask—So why is your daughter not married? takes the cake. I would like to ask those very people. Why? Are you saving money to finance my marriage?

Our country no matter the cultural transformation it boasts of having gone through, has not given woman the equal status yet. If a girl is not married till a particular age, then there is a problem in the girl. If a woman happens to be part of a divorce she surely did something not right. In fact, even when a female is subjected to the horrific crime of rape in India, there will be some loose mouths that will hold the woman responsible in some way over it.

Anyways moving forward, MNC Supplyman calls up on Sunday and that also happens to be the first time we speak. Also that is the first time I notice that he stammers.

This crucial detail was not mentioned in his matrimony profile page. Anyways, I told myself, he might be a perfect man, even if not speech perfect.

I told my dad everything about CAchand over tea that morning. Though he is a proud dad, he is also a worried dad. He too wonders why things are not working in the right direction. But like every time we convince each other they will.

As I get ready to go out and meet MNC Supplyman, an SMS flashes on my phone screen.

God will punish you and you will never be happy—CAchand

I am not surprised. This message certifies that I have judged his character well.

On the way to Starbucks Goregaon, I received a call from Alisha. Neel has spoken to her about yesterday's happening and she congratulates me over what she calls—The Woman's Victory. I tell her about the next meeting. She gives me a reply that cracks me up—if you like him, eat the man. If you don't like him, eat the food. In any case, you eat and he pays the bill.

There is a thing called fearless woman. Alisha is that and more.

Like every day, Starbucks is full of people. I don't know if I picked the right place, but honestly I was not thinking too much and just chose the first venue that came in my mind quite randomly.

I recognized MNC Supplyman the moment I saw him. He looks exactly the same as his picture on the matrimonial website. Trust me, that is a blessing too.

MNC Supplyman—S s s sorry. I am late.

Bengal Rani—No problem. I came a bit early.

MNC Supplyman—You like S s s Starbucks?

Bengal Rani—Most people like Starbucks don't they?

MNC Supplyman—I don't. T t t too crowded.

Bengal Rani—I like fun places.

MNC Supplyman—I don't like parties and nois s se.

Bengal Rani—So tell me about your work.

MNC Supplyman—I work hard. My management t t is s s happy. They are promoting me s s soon.

I notice he had problems with two letters in majority. T and S. The rest seems in control so far.

Bengal Rani—Good to hear.

MNC Supplyman—T t t tell me about your work.

Bengal Rani—I am a marketing communications professional. I basically handle brands and that includes advertising, events, social media, writing and all the jazz that comes along with it.

MNC Supplyman—Event t t? You like nois s se and part t ty?

Bengal Rani—I won't say I am regular with it. But I also won't say I dislike it.

MNC Supplyman—Once my office people want t ted to do a part t ty in a dis s sco. Management wasss joining. Celebration part t ty. I t t told the management I was nottt well and gottt the venue changed. Barbeque Nation.

Bengal Rani—That's bad of you. Weren't your colleagues unhappy?

MNC Supplyman—I don'ttt like p p part t ties. They are nottt my concern.

Bengal Rani—But people like enjoying. You should also be nice to people and allow them to do what they like.

MNC Supplyman—I earn more. I am of more value t t to the company. My wish should be considered firsttt.

I looked at him and waited for an hour to get over. The more I spoke the more I understood his problem. MNC Supplyman was very insecure and in full awareness of his speech problem. And hence he had an aversion against all people with normal speech which comprised most of the people in our society. Also he kept away from places that were more communication prone as those were also the places that would reveal his disability. The saddest part of the story was he wasn't willing to change his perspective. Irritating people and spoiling their plans was his favourite pleasure deriving sport. He was not ashamed of it and wanted to continue this chosen path of life and pity himself.

I pitied him. I felt terrible for him. But I couldn't love him. I knew that in an hour's time.

After an hour was over, I started leaving and looked behind at the mall inside which Starbucks was located. There had been many men I had met to marry. And there are still many who I would meet. Would I continue the way I am or will things finally fall in place? Would life be perfect and normal? Would I really be happy?

I called up my AOL teacher and asked him the same questions. He had the answer to the last question. And gave me an easier route.

Fifteen minutes later, I was laughing my guts out, inside a theatre. Minions outdid both the performances that I had encountered the last two days.

I was ready. For a new week. For newer men. For newer experiences.

Chapter 9
The Perfect Marketer

So you are closer to the end of the book. And the finale man.

Thank you for reading right up till this page. And if you just like me, prefer reading backwards, then that too will be fine. The men don't change. And the experiences only get more awkward. In fact, this one is a serious note.

This is the last of my experiences that I have jotted down for public reading. Not that I was short of stories. But these were the ones that are either shocking, weird, plain stupid or hilarious enough to stay in my memory.

However, this last piece is nothing of all those things. When I started, I actually believed that writing this one would be the easiest. On the contrary, it is turning out to be anything but simple.

If this would have worked, then this book would not have happened. After all, Perfect Marketer is the first matrimonial profile I encountered.

That was two years back.

One Sunday morning, I was reading the newspaper and yawning aimlessly. Sunday mornings are about that. No real plan, no fixed agendas or to dos other than what you will eat, when will you eat, what time you will sleep, when will you sleep, and repeat. I was always very sure that if Saturdays were for the worldly pleasures of party all night, then Sundays are for the more necessary and basic needs of life—eat, gossip and sleep.

Now this is the way it had been and I was hoping that this is the way it would always be. However, fate had a different blueprint for my next few years. And the ones to announce it to me were the two people who I believed were my well-wishers till then.

That fateful morning, my dad and mom conspired to change all my Saturdays and Sundays for what is becoming a long time now.

Sunday mornings in my home were and in fact still are chai pe charcha between mom, dad and beti. There is no one particular topic. We can debate about which political party leader will take route of opposition for which favour, why Mahabharat is more important than Ramayana or vice versa, what is a cat's staple diet, why Madhuri Dixit is prettier than Sridevi according to me, what are the other avenues for Rakhi Sawant to earn her roti, kapda, makaan and surgeries, or why does our neighbour taste his dog's pedigree every day before serving it to him. Today, however, the room was quieter. That is rarely the case in our house. My dad and mom were looking at me, sipping their tea, then browsing through the newspapers and finally again eyeing me.

It gave a bad feeling. You know the one you get when you do something wrong and hide it. But on the contrary, I had been coming home well on time, there was a promotion that everyone was happy about, I had lost weight, I was also going to temples regularly, I was cooking sometimes, I was learning belly dancing…it all seemed perfect. And sober.

Dad (folding his newspaper and giving me a rather hesitant smile)—So, how is life going?

Bengal Rani (I immediately knew there was something much bigger that was to hit me very soon)—Very good. I am happy. Why?

Mom (finally issuing her first statement)—So, is this the life you want to lead?

With whatever I had jotted down, I think I was doing well. That question didn't fit right in my current scheme of things. In fact, that is the question you ask a terrorist in a rehabilitation camp after he has admitted his crime.

Bengal Rani (no choice but to reply)—Is there something wrong with what I am doing with my life?

Dad—No, not at all. It's all good. Don't you think it can be a lot better?

Bengal Rani (that question was an opportunity)—Yes, it can dad, you just said it. Let's do the USA vacation.

Dad (converting my opportunity to his)—Actually, yes you must do the USA vacation. I think it is time.

I was beaming with joy. I had been after dad's life literally for the last two years for this USA vacation and he had dashed my request each time with pain points like finance, grandparents, safety, recession, food and even racism.

Nothing in these two years had however changed significantly for the United States of America. Then what had propped up and changed my dad's decision suddenly on a sunny Sunday morning? I should have been smarter.

Mom (keeping her tea cup on one side of the table and moving closer to sit beside me. There is hardly any place but my mom has this innate ability of accomplishing anything she sets her heart on. She manages)—Beta, you have done such brilliant work. Academics wise you are in a good place for now. But you know something, life will get very lonely after a certain age. You know what I mean?

Now I got it. This was feeding the goat before sacrifice time. They had prepared well. And I knew immediately what would be my dad's next line.

Dad (excited, elated, mad)—Here is an idea. You get married and I shall gift you a fifteen day trip to USA with your brand new husband! How does that sound?

Brand new husband! That sounded hilarious and like the latest jacket I had picked. Though as time passed, I was able to find very close similarities between the two actions.

Bengal Rani (thinking fast but off ideas totally; what to do, what to do, what to do)—You think it's time?

Mom—You were six by now when I was your age.

Bengal Rani—Your times were different.

Mom—Exactly why you don't have a six-year-old kid of your own by now.

They were hell bent. I had to do it. They had all the reasons. I had to do it. They were not wrong. I had to do it. There was no harm trying. I had to do it. Things could be bad. I had to do it. Things could be great. I had to do it. If I disliked it, I had to do it. If I was going to enjoy it, I had to do it.

So I did it. My profile for matrimonial listing was ready.

I had never seen my mom more excited in my life. For me, it was plain fun. For her, it was a different accomplishment of sorts. So started the profile building which in my view could have been simpler and not as detailed. But there were questions to fill and certain mandatory ones. As I started entering my height, weight, salary, etc. a fleeting thought crossed my head. All of this put up here could as well be fake. Is it really that difficult for any individual to put up wrong details about him/her and fake it further for many more meetings? Authentication of details is possible only till a certain limit. And if someone is up to mischief and well-planned mischief, let me tell you the probability and risks, both are on the higher side.

However, I did not lie about anything big or small. As good or as bad.

Thus began my online matrimonial yatra. And the moment the final click was done; the army of eligible bachelors landed on my father's laptop. I was very sure that I would not do any of this activity on my own for the fear of addresses getting stored and popping up to embarrass me while me and friends were playing UK Top 100 on my machine.

Honestly this started with fun. There were so many guys. A lot in my own city and some living far away in foreign countries. Many ex IITs, ex IIMs, Senior Vice Presidents, CAs, Doctors, name it and they were there.

However my eyes were fixed sharp on one profile only. I am in the field of Marketing. So a fellow marketer is always a more respected entity in my world. And that respect multiplies a million times if he is good looking, tall enough, well dressed and heads marketing in one of the top entertainment conglomerates of India. To top it, he was the quintessential Mumbai person and had stayed in the city since toddler days.

If there was a match, this it was.

But I didn't react. I wanted to experiment with this tool called online matrimony and see how it works first. So that day, we did not send out any interests. The next morning though my mom was jumping with joy. Many interests had arrived for me and well, even if many of them were not the right match for me, some were. The best news of the day was that Perfect Marketer had sent me an interest. Now I could call the day well begun.

A day or two passed and communication began on various fronts, while my head was stuck to Perfect Marketer. That was the only number that had not blinked on my dad's mobile yet. I shrugged my shoulders many times a day consoling myself over it.

Then three days later while we were redoing our organization's website's homepage, dad called me with some good news.

"Congrats, his father called. They are coming home on Saturday."

Gosh, such a relief! Finally, the man of my dreams had been found and he would be here soon. Needless to say I had by now gone through his Facebook profile and was able to see few things though majority was hidden courtesy privacy settings. I liked people who did that. Keeping things exclusive was such a wonderful mark of class.

So the first matrimonial proposal was coming home. It was all exciting and sensational suddenly. Maybe because the more I investigated about Perfect Marketer, the more I liked him. He seemed very apt and husband material.

By the way, what is husband material? Every girl would have a different answer to that by all means. For some, it is the man who gave her all his time. For some, it would mean the man who cooked her Sunday breakfasts and surprised her with her favourite recipes whenever he was free. There were few for whom husband material was proportional to how much the man cared for her parents and how good a father he would be.

For me, it was none of these. I did not expect time or a masterchef. I of course would love my husband getting along well with my folks; however, overdoing isn't exactly my thing. My husband material is the man I can have conversations all my life with happily. And by what Perfect Marketer was doing with his life, it was clear I would enjoy listening to him and there would be plenty of words, in spite of limited time.

Mom that evening with her handbook of preparations made a beeline to my room. *Heabi planning* as we say in Bengalish accent.

Mom—So we need to go pick up an Indian dress for you.

Bengal Rani—But mom, I have plenty.

Mom—They are all old.

Bengal Rani—No mom, there is enough here. I don't see a reason we pick anymore.

Mom—No, you will not wear old clothes. This is the first proposal. You will only wear new and bright clothes. A very pretty churidar kurta in pink should do.

Sometimes arguing doesn't help. Moreover, she would spend and I would have one more Indian suit in my wardrobe. Why revolt!

Mom—And food? What should be the menu you think?

Bengal Rani—Order some samosas and make some canapés if possible. Tea to go with it.

Mom (freaking out)—Are you mad? We are Bengalis. Cultural Bengalis! Have you forgotten that we display our goodness with our food? No. Samosas and canapés are for poor people. I will have something better to go on the plate.

Bengal Rani—Which is?

Mom—Mmm…let me see. Okay, chicken kheema cutlets and paneer pakodas. Both served with mayo dip and green mint coriander chutney. How's that?

Again, guests who visited in the evening occupied a special place in my heart. Great snacks were prepared for them and served in snack like portions and finally when they left all of that was served to us family members in dinner like proportions. So, why revolt!

Finally, the menu and the clothes for the day were settled. The shopping happened the very next day and though pink could not make it till my home that evening, purple did and it was beautiful.

Friday morning, I called up my dear friend Karishma and informed her about the latest big thing in my life. Now this latest big thing was an on-going activity in Karishma's life since college and she was mentally quite done with it. It hardly excited her. But the moment Karishma, the HR professional heard the name of the prospective groom, she jumped.

Karishma—Perfect Marketer? Really? Really Perfect Marketer? Really?

Bengal Rani (calming the friend)—Yes Perfect Marketer. Why are you sounding like you have been put on a hot frying pan?

Karishma—Dude! You don't know what this is! Oh my God, darling this is news. Mr Perfect Marketer is one of the most eligible bachelors around. Wait, I have to tell Chelsea. Chelseaaa…guess what! Bengal Rani is marrying Perfect Marketer.

Bengal Rani (hearing hoooooos and haaaas in the phone)—Hold on. His parents are visiting. Nothing final here.

Karishma—Isn't that half the battle won already? They will love you, you know that.

Bengal Rani—No guarantee. How can you be so sure?

Karishma—We went to the same college. Would I not know that you were liked by most? Bengal Rani—Those days were different babes. You know times have changed and life too has.

Karishma (being the more positive one like always)—Bengal Rani hasn't. She is still as amazing as she used to be.

We both laughed to that. Karishma and I had finished graduation together and that had been perhaps the most wonderful times of our lives. We were one happy lot. All of us in fact. There were so many then and in every sense, it was fantastic. It still is, but that was a more carefree party.

So armed with the friend's good luck, I marched forward. However, one last thing was needed to boost my confidence. A chat with my Art of Living teacher. I had known him for years now and a true transformation of my life towards better health and better living had happened through Art Of Living or AOL as they called it. I was not the devotional religion seeker. I was the healing and good health seeker. And my AOL teacher recognized my needs and did just that for me from time to time.

AOL Teacher—Just be. Don't get over excited or worked up.

Bengal Rani—I know. But I would love this working out, that's it.

AOL Teacher—So let it happen. Don't run.

Bengal Rani—What do you think?

AOL Teacher—Why think? I will tell you again what I told you when we met, when you lost your first job and today when we started talking. Just be. Eventually it all falls in place. It always has.

Bengal Rani—Yes it has. You are right.

AOL Teacher—So breathe in, breathe out, calm and just be.

It wasn't as easy as it sounded. But it did work nonetheless and each time. Whatever you cry for, gives you more tears. Hence, one needs to stop associating emotion to it and let it all happen. Do your efforts and let life flow. As time passed I realized, that not just Art of Living but every major religion or spiritual cult in our world which saw miracles and manifestation followed the simple formula of what they called the laws of attraction or the laws of cause and effect or sometimes the more popular Karma.

I was a lucky student, but a slow learner. Thankfully, my teachers have had great patience.

So when Sunday evening finally arrived and the doorbell rung, I chose to not panic. This was the first of its sort meeting. I had no experience in it. Meeting the parents of a guy who I had never met but was ready to marry.

Sounds so absurd. Welcome to the east!

Sitting in the bedroom, I decoded that the father was the more talkative one. The mother was the control freak. The father was all accepting. The mother was all judging. The father loved to eat. The mother checked her own and his diet. Basically, I had to make sure that the father liked me and the mother loved me.

Fifteen minutes passed and then suddenly the war cry was sounded. I was called. Breathe in, breathe out. Breathe in, Breathe out. Ommmmm...Okay moment of test, here I come.

Immediately the head dive one each for the mother and the father. Commonly known as pranaam in India. Everybody in India older than you deserves a pranaam. Doesn't matter what they do in life. You don't use logic in matters of pranaam.

Perfect Marketer's mother—(lightly trying to stop me) Okay okay, you don't need to do that.

Every elderly person in India says this line, once the pranaam act is over.

Perfect Marketer's father—How are you beta? And you have such a beautiful home. I am already loving it. Perfect Marketer will love it too.

Bengal Rani (sitting on the couch with back straight and alert position)—Thank you so much uncle.

Perfect Marketer's father—And I can promise you, that when you visit our home I shall not be able to give you such wonderful cutlets. These are so delicious.

Mom—Thank you so much. I shall get you some more. Just wait for five minutes.

Perfect Marketer's mother—(gaining control)—Please don't. He has high BP. Not right for him at all.

Perfect Marketer's father—What is the point of cooking great food if guests are not allowed to eat it? But what to do? Women have more power in this country than men!

There is laughter in the room and the mood lightens further. There is a hidden clue I think in what the father said about us visiting their home. Maybe I have passed the test.

Then there are more questions. About education, work timings, Perfect Marketer's life in general, my culinary skills and their comparison with mom's and finally the session moves to a round of our house.

They are impressed with the house too. Another brownie point earned.

Finally the end of the evening arrives and everyone is smiling. Smiling a lot. Perfect Marketer's father hands over his son's number to me and informs me of his pet name. Will it help so soon, I have my doubts.

Anyways once they left, mom and dad looked happy and satisfied. It has been a good meeting and from the sound of it, looks highly positive. I too feel great about it. They both were encouraging and nice people. I would have been happier if Perfect Marketer had arrived too, but since he didn't, let's leave that for now and talk to him the next day.

Monday blues are not really blue this morning. I have been digging the World Wide Web further and collecting crucial information about Mr Perfect Marketer. Chanced on a couple of his interviews and my belief about him being perfect intensifies further.

With this belief, I dialled his number.

No answer.

Never mind. The day has just begun.

It is 12 pm and there is no call on my phone. I get frustrated a bit too soon and notice me clenching my fists. Not fun.

But wait a minute. I never left a message for him to know who was calling him today morning. Maybe I should just do that.

'Dear Perfect Marketer, this is Bengal Rani. Your dad passed on your number to me. Let me know if you are free to speak. Cheers.'

An hour passes and no reply comes. Now I am getting tensed further. I started calling my friends to pacify my nerves and tell Karishma about it. The moron gives me the Just be line.

Next caller.

I dialled Neel. He disconnected my call and messaged me—In a meeting. Give an hour.

Next caller.

Arshi's number was busy. I disconnected and called her again. Busy. Again called her. Still busy.

Now I wanted to tear my hair. Has the entire world decided to boycott me!

Then like divine intervention, my phone rings. And you know what, I do the happy dance. It is Mr. Perfect Marketer.

Bengal Rani—Hello

Perfect Marketer—Hey hi. How are you?

Bengal Rani—Hi, I am good. Sorry if I bothered you.

Perfect Marketer—No not really ya. Just that there is our film Bands of Sons releasing in two weeks. So the director Anupam Kashi has been calling day in and day out. So yes, I have been keeping the phone free as much.

Bengal Rani—I understand. How were you anyways?

Perfect Marketer—Well, just as good. By the way dad told me that you have a very beautiful and artistic house.

Bengal Rani—You must visit sometime. You would like it too.

Perfect Marketer—Definitely definitely. But first let these three projects get over.

Bengal Rani (wondering the duration of it)—Oh, are they really long?

Perfect Marketer—Actually kind of but not very long. Till November. We are sitting in June right now. November is light years away.

Bengal Rani—Get it. Anyways, I too have a meeting. So let's catch up later.

Perfect Marketer—Sure there. Nice talking to you. Bye.

When I am not happy or not winning in a conversation, I just buy time. The November detail was not fitting well.

But like the heart of a newly in love idiot is, I focused on the good things. His voice wasn't particularly bad. He was to some extent friendly. And of course he was a very successful man. Perfect husband material remember.

So the next few days we whatsapped. Not much though, but we did. The basic know each other chat. He was busy all the time and quite a content guy. Very modest and rarely opinionated.

I suggested we meet and after some dilly dallying we decided the day and venue.

Costa Coffee Juhu was the lucky cafeteria to witness my first online matrimony meeting or date or whatever.

Two stupid things happened in Costa Coffee that evening. I got stuck in the washroom thanks to a highly dysfunctional lock. And Perfect Marketer witnessed my struggle with it.

So it was a shabby start. But never mind there was always time to recover. And try again.

Perfect Marketer—Hey how are you?

Bengal Rani—I am not very bad. You just saw that. Not a very good start.

Perfect Marketer—Chill ya…all that keeps happening. Sit and relax. Should I get you something?

Bengal Rani—A little later would be nice.

Perfect Marketer—Actually I am a hungry.

Bengal Rani (happy to have found a fellow food fan)—Okay, let's go and order something to eat.

Few minutes later we were back on our tables with my Chicken kidney beans puff and his carrot cake.

Bengal Rani (nibbling into the food)—So tell me, the movies business. Must be interesting.

Perfect Marketer—It is in a way. See I always liked it. And with my face, I couldn't be a hero, so became what I am.

Bengal Rani—Oh come on, you look very good.

Perfect Marketer—Ya, but not hero nice. Moreover age. Anyways, no complaints except that the salary could have been a tad better.

He earned a fantastic salary. But like the rest of corporate India, he too believed that he was overworked and underpaid. Anyways we laughed and I suggested that in terms of money, my story and thoughts are very similar.

Bengal Rani—Your father mentioned you travel a lot.

Perfect Marketer—Some hard selling he did hasn't he?

Bengal Rani—Yes, he speaks more in favour of you than your mom.

Perfect Marketer (blushing this time)—Yes dad is happy with what I do. I like travelling. Done my bit. Italy, France, a lot of Europe, some parts of India.

Bengal Rani—Sounds wonderful. Italy is on my list too. I have a thing for history.

Perfect Marketer—Then you should visit Italy. Museums, cathedrals and much more. Of course great food to top that.

The conversation flows and there is a lot we speak of. In fact, I didn't realize that an hour just passed by. Perfect Marketer is someone I can keep having conversations with.

Oh bless me again. Perfect Husband Material.

Suddenly my Perfect Husband Material looks at his watch. And remembers that he needs to finish a meeting with the heroine of the next film the media conglomerate he is working for. She happens to also be the producer of the film and is the nasty, abusive sort. So he better be on time.

Perfect Marketer (as we leave the coffee shop)—I would have dropped you home. But I need to rush really.

Bengal Rani—No worries, I will manage.

Perfect Marketer—It was nice meeting you. Had a great time.

Bengal Rani—Same here. Bye.

That evening when I was coming home, I was not able to decide whether I had won or lost the game. Had he liked me or disliked me. Was I a pass or a fail or simply put was I the Perfect Wife Material for the Perfect Marketer?

I dialled all the numbers I used to anyways dial to gain clarity and each gave me different answers. Only time will tell was the final writing on the wall.

Three weeks passed by and though we spoke there wasn't really much fire in the conversation. Perfect Marketer was a busy man. I didn't have a problem with that of course. But he was what he was.

Fourth week, I received a message from him.

'Hi Bengal Rani, you are a wonderful girl and everything is right with you. However, I am at the moment very busy and am not being able to concentrate and give time to this entire process. I am running very busy till November. So I suggest we let things be and then if you are still around we can then pick up the strings from where we left them behind and see if we can work it together.'

I won't lie. That message wasn't what I wanted to read. I did break my heart in some way. But the reality of the day was exactly those words. My Perfect husband material wasn't ready to be that. Atleast not yet.

I gave a rather let's please him reply.

'Hey Perfect Marketer, I am indeed honoured that you were able to say this to me. I totally understand your point of view and it's completely alright if you need that kind of time. We shall go by what you choose and hopefully things will be better.'

I informed my folks. And the journey for my perfect husband hit the restart button.

Much later, Perfect Marketer informed me that it was not me, but the idea of marriage that he was shy off. He was not ready for marriage then and he was not sure if he would ever be. His online matrimonial listing was his parents idea and not his own. He was just being put into it because he had not really found somebody special enough to walk the aisle with. In fact surprisingly, I was the only girl he ever met through online matrimony.

At that time I offered him the option of meeting more often and giving things a chance but he politely said—What is the point in fanning emotions, going astray and not giving such pure feelings the respect and place they deserve?

It would have been great if things would have worked. To me he was everything I wanted. However, maybe to him I was not everything he wanted or mostly he was not looking for companionship.

Till date, whenever I have asked him for any help he has offered it unfailingly. He has always been pleasant and courteous. Considering the circumstances we met in, we could perhaps either be husband wife or nothing. Or maybe we could have been friends. Not just friends but the ones you identify as your twin soul sometimes. Or maybe if we had met causally at a party then perhaps we could have had a matrimony baggage free conversation. Again maybe if I had met him over a job interview then he might have been the boss, the mentor, a guide and who knows a friend too.

So many maybes. But then life has its plans.

So the last and the most important story of my matrimonial journey ends. And surprisingly this was the first. The time I felt that I genuinely missed out on a very amazing man.

All said and done, life goes on. And I am sure we all are destined to be where we should really be.

So Mr Perfect Marketer, I wish you all the luck in finding your perfect wife, perfect work, perfect vacation, perfect companion, perfect home, or whatever matters to you.

May life be perfect with you.

Chapter 10
Why and Now What

So these were the top nine of my matrimonial journeys. Why nine, because I hear it is the most successful number and my astrological surroundings have unfortunately started intruding my thinking. Eesh!

When I started writing, I think few weeks back, I thought I was the only one. However, these few weeks and a little bit of talking has alerted me that there are many many many more, just like me.

For everyone who is currently insecure, hasn't met their idle partner or is going through a breakup or is perhaps just lost and unable to find direction, I suggest you to go and get a fish pedicure done. You know why? The therapy will expose you to the one fact of life, which we all conveniently forget in our moments of desperation and sorry.

There are many fish in the pond.

Now, I do not endorse the belief that matrimonial sites are bad and no one has ever gained out of them. I am sure many today are living the most beautiful time of their lives thanks to these tools. However, let's not forget that like every technology, this too is not fool proof. There are enough fake profiles floating online which one needs to bear caution against. Also while many feel that he or she is the only one stuck up and unable to move ahead with someone and on the verge of an unhappy compromise, wait a minute. There are many more just like you. It is just that everybody does not know everybody. And failures are rarely discussed. We speak of great love stories and happy marriages. How many hate stories or emotional catastrophes find way till people's reading palettes. Nobody likes reading a sad story. We are also living in the culture of commercialization of positivity with a lot of our writing moving to the power of happy thoughts and its ability to change destiny. I sanction that thought. This book is a product of the very motivation created by the "'thoughts become things' faith.

But somebody needs to write and speak of the not so nice things, the stuck up things, the things that will hopefully be right and the things that look like they will never be right. These nine stories are my way of telling the girls and mind you the guys too because they also often go through this grind and females are equally capable of being menacing, two simple key points. There is hope. And you are not wrong. Morons exist in our society and if you have met or are meeting plenty of them one after another, at marathon speed, it is okay and chances are that many more will come your way. Chill. Just be.

This too shall pass. That's god's word not mine.

The right one will come along.

Till then, love your parents because sometimes what they do is not their fault. Let your aunts, uncles, grand moms, nephews, nieces and all those who are troubling you with unwarranted questions be forgiven. Think like Jesus and say—Forgive them my Lord. They don't know what they do.

Don't look down upon happy marriages. Wish them more happiness. Also know that a lot of times, a lot of things are just a cover. I leave it to that.

Work, enhance your career, make money, eat what you love, buy what you wish to own, take that road trip or luxury vacation, and do the charity you always hoped to do. Also do yourself one mandatory favour. Love yourself. More than anything else in this world.

Happiness is the only way to be.

At the end of every matrimonial meeting gone wrong I tell myself that. I also see that most meetings fail not because I am any less of a nice person. It is because two people are compatible. Or not compatible.

Yes I call a few of those who I met dumb or worthless or chauvinist. All these names are signs of incompatibility. Chill, the right match is right there for you and it has its time to show up.

So I sign off here. There will be more stories and more experiences till finally the day when I do not need to write them down. And if you have any that you want the world to know you may write to me at the email address mentioned behind the book. I will voice them for you. A people's sequel is not a bad idea at all. It might make me some money too (giggles).

So this is me signing off for now.

Wish you Love, Happiness, Experiences Always

Bengal Rani